THE FINAL GAME

David B. Smith

REVIEW AND HERALD® PUBLISHING ASSOCIATION
HAGERSTOWN, MD 21740

The author assumes full responsibility for the accuracy
of all facts and quotations as cited in this book.

This book was
Edited by Gerald Wheeler
Cover design by Willie S. Duke
Cover illustration by Peter Ambush
Typeset: 10/12 Optima

PRINTED IN U.S.A.

01 00 99 98 97   10 9 8 7 6 5 4 3 2 1

R&H Cataloging Service
Smith, David B
    The final game.

    I. Title.

        813.54

ISBN 0-8280-1287-3

DEDICATION

For *my* Lisa

CHAPTER 1

TELEVISION
LIGHTS

The flushed sportscaster cocked his head to one side, adjusting his earpiece. The hot light over the remote TV camera caused tiny beads of sweat to dot his forehead. "On in three," the producer grunted, counting down.

"Well, folks, we're here live at courtside at the high school where our Hampton High Panthers just finished—as anticipated—a 13-and-3 season." "Big Max" had been a regular fixture at the last two home games, both big blowout wins for the varsity squad. "And Bucky Stone, always in the thick of things here during what we call Panther Pandemonium . . . you had another outstanding game tonight." He shoved the microphone in the tall athlete's face.

Bucky grinned. "Thanks. The whole team had a pretty good night."

The older man hesitated for just a moment. "All around the district, people are saying that this is a team that just can't be beat. You fellows came back from Hawaii where you *didn't* win the invitational. But somehow that tournament kind of kicked you men into high gear. Five straight wins plus the three wins from before—that's a pretty hot eight in a row heading into the playoffs. Tell us right here: *can* anybody beat the Panthers?"

The athlete shook his head. "Well, we're playing about as good as I can remember. And once we got Volker back, Coach told us we didn't really have any excuses after that."

Just out of range, Dan Litton made a face at him. "I want to get on TV too!" he whispered loudly. "Say something about Litton. *Dan* Litton!" Bucky tried not to laugh.

"There have been a few stories in the paper where you're really the one who holds this team together," Max went on. "That after Bill came back to the team, you went to him and kind of patched things up. And of course, with your, you know, religious experience and everything." He hesitated. "Any comment?"

The *live*ness of the moment gave Bucky a prickly feeling. "Well, Dan and I play for God," he said simply. "I mean, that's all there is to it. So when Bill came back, I just went to him and said, 'Bygones are bygones, Volker. Let's go undefeated the rest of the way.' And he's been marvelous to play with."

The TV reporter gave a little nod, accepting the words. "Well, whatever you guys have going in that locker room, it's working big-time. Best of luck to you in the playoffs, Bucky."

Max faced the camera. "For News at 10:00, this is 'Big Max' with all the big stories. Back to you, Donny."

Dan came over and feigned a little kick at his teammate's shins. "You're the biggest camera hog in California," he complained. "Couldn't you work me in at all?"

"I did!" Bucky protested. "Didn't you hear me? I said something like, 'Dan and I play for God.' See? '*Dan* and I.' Last I checked, that was you."

"Oh yeah." Chastised, the stocky forward managed a

grin. "Let's grab a shower, shorty. Wash some of that star-dust out of your hair."

The hot water felt good—especially after eight wins in a row. Still, he felt something disquieting about the air of invincibility that permeated the hallways and basketball arena of Hampton Beach High. He sidled over to where Dan was still lathering up. "You think this whole playoff is as automatic for us as everybody says?"

Dan shrugged, rinsing some soap out of his face before answering. "Beats me. We've clobbered every team in the league. And with Billy Boy, we'd have gone 16 and 0. But still, anything can happen."

"I know. I'm kind of worried that everyone's so, I don't know . . . complacent."

"Yeah." Dan eased down the water pressure a bit so he could hear. In the far corner Bill and Jonesy were screaming at each other good-naturedly about some botched play that wasn't anybody's fault. "Look, all we can do is play hard like we've done all along. Just don't let us get complacent. We've got the best coaching and the best starting five. If the baskets drop, we're going to win. After that, we just play for God like always." He laughed. "Like *you* said on nationwide TV."

Bucky starting laughing. "Oh, right. Nationwide. Big Max probably has all of 50 viewers on that podunk station."

The winter night air was cold as they left the athletic complex. With the last contest being such an automatic win, Bucky's parents had finally skipped a game. He fumbled for his car keys. "Julie didn't come tonight?"

The older boy shook his head. "Nah. She knew we'd win by 9,000 points, so she said she was going to work. She'll come to all the playoffs, though."

"Litton finally has a girlfriend." Bucky bumped his teammate's leg with his duffel bag. "It's about time."

The new romance had been sparking along well for about

three weeks now. Julie, a medium-height senior with tight curly hair and a big laugh, matched Dan's ebullient sense of humor well. "Not an Adventist but a real decent Christian" was how he'd described her, and she'd already visited the Adventist church with him and Dan once. It was funny how after three and a half years of going to the same high school, Dan and Julie had suddenly "noticed" each other shortly after the Panthers returned home from their Hawaii adventure.

"Next Monday we're playing for real." Dan's face suddenly turned sober. "Man, I really want to finish champs at this place." He looked around at the nearly deserted campus. "Plus in baseball too."

Bucky nodded. Next year he'd be at an Adventist college with Dan and Sam, so this was a kind of final opportunity to participate in sports at such an advanced level. Both keenly felt the desire to win in a way that their commitment to Jesus would be obvious to those who watched. Was it possible that their senior year might include back-to-back championships? Friday night games in baseball had kept them off the varsity squad last season. But inexplicably, the basketball playoff schedule was a beautiful Monday-Thursday-Monday setup that was perfect for the two young Christians.

He sat for a moment in the little white Toyota, thinking, as Dan's sports car gunned into the darkness. The euphoria of being the sparkplug of such a hot basketball team this school year was tempered by a continuing loneliness that still tugged at him. Since Hawaii, he'd seen Lisa only once as she drove out of the high school student parking lot. She had given him a little wave, kind of a wistful gesture.

Mom and Dad were sitting around the kitchen table, enjoying a rare game of Scrabble, when he came in. "Hey, champ." Dad plunked down three letters and sniffed impatiently as he counted up the meager points. "You guys win, I assume?"

"Yeah." Bucky took a quick peek at the playing board, which was hopelessly crowded on the bottom half. "Pretty gummed up, looks like."

"It's your mother's fault. I set her up about three times, and she puts down words like 'cat.' So it's all crowded down there." His father picked the three remaining game pieces out of the pile and pretended to scowl at them. "Horrible. I haven't had a good letter all night. So how much you beat 'em by?"

"I don't know. About 15."

"All right. Skunk City. You boys ready for the playoffs?"

"I guess so." He paused. "Is Rachel Marie asleep yet?"

Mom shook her head, fumbling with her last letters as she did so. "Are you kidding? It's getting harder and harder to get her to bed. She just went about 10 minutes ago."

Bucky put his gear in the closet. "I'll go see her for just a minute then."

It was dark upstairs, and he quietly felt his way down the hallway. Even as a fourth-grader, his sister still liked having a small night light, and he could see the soft glow coming through under the door to her room. He tapped lightly on the door and then went in. "Hey, short person."

"Hi."

Fritzie the Bear was perched on the pillow next to her. He reached over and nudged the stuffed animal back into place. "How was school today?"

"Good." Her voice was drowsy. "Did you and Dan win?"

"We sure did." He leaned down and kissed her. "And we dedicated the victory to Miss Rachel Marie Stone, the beautiful sister of the all-star forward."

"Did you really? Cool!" Then she frowned at him. "You didn't really, did you?"

"Well . . . sort of. In my mind, we did." He grinned. "Just now, that is."

He kissed her again. "I love you, I guess."

"Me too." Her eyes were already closed as he edged toward the door.

Round One in the basketball tourney started out harder than the hometown Panthers had anticipated. The varsity team from Milpitas, as outclassed as they were on paper, and with just a 9-7 record, held the Hampton Beach squad in check during the first half, and even led by a pair of baskets late in the game. Jonesy Wilson, in particular, was having an off night, missing several easy layups. But Brayshaw's players, after a tense time out with five minutes left, managed to come back and win by five points.

It was a sober team that showered after the game. "I told you," Bucky warned Dan as they toweled off. "We're not as invincible as everyone thinks."

Obviously concerned as well, Coach Brayshaw called an extra practice for Tuesday afternoon, and ran the team through it as if it was preseason. "Come on, come on, come on!" he shouted during the endless rebound drills. "Box somebody out! Put a body on him!"

Ironically, the Thursday semifinal game was easy compared to the previous squeaker. The Panthers came screaming out of the chute and scored nine unanswered points, including a long-range three-pointer from Bill Volker. The stunned Tornadoes tried to come back midway through the half, but Hampton's lead never dipped below 14 points. The comfortable home crowd cheered amiably with every Panther basket. However, the game lacked the usual intensity of a playoff do-or-die contest.

"That's more like it," Dan grinned, accepting a kiss from Julie outside the locker room. "Like taking candy from a baby."

"Yeah, but now we're complacent again," Bucky grumbled as the three of them walked toward Dan's Camaro. "How're we going to get psyched up again for Monday?"

"Hey, that's the finals," his friend asserted. "I'll have no problem getting excited about that one. Last chance for a championship ring, Stone." He looked over at Julie. "Shall we invite our lonely friend to go out for ice cream with us?"

"That's OK," Bucky responded. "My folks are waiting for me. Plus I'd just be in the way."

"That's true, you would." Dan started laughing and gave his girlfriend a nudge. "I was afraid he'd think we really wanted him to come."

Riding home in the back seat with Rachel Marie, he thought briefly about Lisa and their freshman year. Their romantic moments of celebration after games had been part of the fun. The three intervening years seemed like an eternity now.

It was a quiet Sabbath at church that weekend. Sam was still away at PUC, and Dan had called him earlier that morning complaining of a sore throat. "Yeah, I'll be fine for Monday night," he told Bucky. "It's just a little bit raw, though, and I don't want to take chances." Bucky sat with Mom and Rachel Marie, listening intently to Pastor Jensen's sermon on winning battles with Satan. "We have a couple of athletes who are playing a pretty big game Monday," the silver-haired minister suddenly interjected, looking over at Bucky's pew. "And for months they've trained. They've sacrificed some of the things they'd probably like to do, so they'll have every possible edge against a very effective opponent." He smiled. "And the same is true in our Christian experience."

Monday evening the Hampton Beach gymnasium was packed for the big final game against Vallejo. Because of a quirk in the schedule, the Panthers had played the visiting team only once during the past two seasons, but Coach Brayshaw had managed to scout out their strengths and weaknesses. "If we stick to our game plan, I guarantee we'll beat 'em," he told the white-clad players in the locker room just before the opening buzzer. He glanced over at Dan and Bucky. "And I know some of you men want to win this last game real bad. Well, me too. Believe me."

The two Christian athletes had just the briefest moment to pray before walking out on the playing floor. "This may be our last opportunity, Lord," Dan prayed. "Help us to witness for You right here."

After the first half of play, a sign in the stands seemed to say it all. "It's So Easy!" Vallejo was having an off night and hardly seemed like championship opponents. The hometown Panthers led by a stunning 18 points, and could easily have been up by more except for a couple of sloppy plays right before the buzzer.

"Don't let up, though!" Coach Brayshaw appeared confident, but you could never tell. An 18-point lead could instantly evaporate in varsity competition. "Let's crush these guys so bad they'll be scared of Hampton Beach for the next 10 years."

Bucky and Dan both got to rest for a good share of the second half as the athletic director shuttled players in and out of the lineup. But with just four minutes left to go and the contest safely "in the refrigerator," he motioned toward the pair. "Get back in there and enjoy yourselves," he grinned. "I want my all-stars to finish."

It was a beautiful end to a great season, Bucky decided, as he dropped a short eight-footer with just a few seconds left. He'd scored only nine points in the game because of the limited playing time, but the whole team was glowing over the easy win. The nearly full gymnasium gave the Panthers a standing ovation.

Several reporters were waiting in the locker room, and TV cameras had been set up, but it wasn't the wild media scene Hampton Beach had experienced the year before with the monster win over the Tornadoes. Still, it was a

good half an hour before the two Christian athletes managed to get to the showers.

"Somebody finally interviewed me," Dan grinned,
washing some soap out of his hair. "I'm almost as famous
as you, Stone." They both laughed, savoring the success
and the nearly four years of shared athletic achievements.

"I gotta confess, I'll miss some of this stuff next year at
PUC," Bucky said at last as they dried off.

"Yeah." Dan shrugged. "Well, they have some sports."

"Not like this, though."

"You're right." The stocky boy winced as a sore muscle
announced its presence. "Well, we weren't such big stars
that we were going to get drafted by the Bulls anyway."

Julie was waiting patiently when the two players finally
emerged. "There she is." Dan grinned. "How 'bout a kiss
from a legend on the court, little girl?"

She laughed and tilted her head toward him. Dan looked
over at his teammate. "Stone, man, get yourself a girlfriend
so we can go out to celebrate like a regular foursome."

"Yeah, who?"

"Take your pick. Tracy. Lisa. That little Thai girl,
what's-her-name, from southern California."

"Vasana?"

"Yeah, her."

Bucky felt a twinge of jealousy as he looked over at
Julie. "That's OK. I'm saving all my romantic prowess for
college." He glanced back into the nearly empty high
school gymnasium, realizing again that he and Litton had
played their final basketball game as Panthers.

"What are you looking at?" Dan came around from the
other side of his car and looked through the open double
doors. Coach Brayshaw was deep in conversation with a
pair of older men, who were both gesturing animatedly.

CHAPTER 2

A CHANGE
OF LEADERSHIP

Even though it was a school night, Bucky treated himself to a bit of late-night television that evening. The 11:00 news replayed the quickie interview he'd had with Max Teufeld, and also some of the footage from the locker room. Then before going upstairs he watched a bit of Jay Leno and flipped though the cable lineup a couple times.

He sat on the edge of the bed praying for a few minutes before climbing in, thanking God for giving him the chances to play ball and be a witness for his Adventist faith. But he couldn't help wonder, even as he prayed, if somehow he might have one last chance to participate in varsity baseball as well. "Lord, I'll do it if You open up the way," he vowed. Again he asked God to bless Lisa, then said a quick amen and tossed his socks in the corner of the room.

In the darkness he lay awake thinking about the senior girl. Although he hardly ever saw Lisa anymore, it had been a habit lately to mention her in his prayers. He wasn't quite sure why.

The next day at school they announced the cancellation of fifth-period classes for a rally in the gym. "We're going to be heroes," Dan laughed, tossing books into his locker. "This is your big chance to get a woman, Stone. Better comb your hair."

"Shut up." Bucky shook his head, bemused. "You get one girlfriend, Litton, and you've had her for all of four weeks now. And all of a sudden, you're the Casanova of Hampton with your stupid advice."

"You got it, shorty."

A big banner stretched across the entire front of the stage area. "Our Varsity Champion Panthers!" it declared. The place was nearly filled with students, and Bucky noticed a lone television crew setting up close to the stage.

Mr. Salomon, the vice principal, was a tall, balding man with a keen sense of humor. "These victory parties are becoming a great way of life around here," he said into the microphone. Cheers and whistles greeted his statement.

Ted Brayshaw came out to another burst of applause. "Back to back, Teddy Bear!" one of the football players in the back hollered out.

The coach managed a grin, but seemed a bit ill at ease. "Let's bring the players up." One by one, Brayshaw listed the names, starting with the subs. "These guys really contributed this year," he told the student body, his amplified words bouncing off the concrete walls. "Give them a big hand."

Bucky tingled as the coach finally read the names of the starting five. "With a JV title his sophomore year and now two straight varsity championships, forward Bucky Stone!" He could feel his face burning a bit as he trotted up and gave Volker, Litton, Scott, and Jonesy Wilson high fives. "And here's our mayor with a special trophy to hand out."

The town's mayor was a chunky African-American businessman who had the reputation for being an avid sports enthusiast. "I almost lost my voice screaming last night," he told the students, pretending to be hoarse. "We're really proud of our high school and its winning tradition." He glanced over at the squad. "Thank you, Coach Brayshaw, for a marvelous job all season. And I'm delighted to be able to come here and deliver the league MVP trophy to our own Mr. Big, the tower of terror, the dominating dynamo of doom, the main man, the block of steel, our all-star center in the middle, Mr. Moses Jones Wilson."

Jonesy started laughing as the names rolled out. "I'm gonna hear about that one," he told Dan as he went forward and received the large trophy with a wave to the student body.

"And here are your varsity awards," the vice principal added, distributing one of the ribboned medallions to each of the players. "Congratulations, guys."

Later at lunch with Dan, Bucky fingered the ornate trophy hanging around his neck. "Adventist jewelry," he laughed.

Dan chewed thoughtfully on his sandwich. "Well, we may get one last chance to play around here. Baseball, I mean."

Bucky pondered that. "You mean, like, frosh ball. Come on, Dan, we're not going to play on the freshman team when we're seniors."

"No, you're right." Taking another bite, Dan swallowed before responding. "But look how the playoff schedule worked out for us. Monday, Thursday, Monday. No sweat. Maybe we'd get lucky with varsity too. No Friday night games or something. Who knows?" He glanced at Bucky's cookies. "Are you going to eat those?"

"Yes." Bucky picked them up and took a quick bite out of both of them at the same time. "Well, after what we've

all been through with Brayshaw and winning two championships, I guess he'd do just about anything he could to get
us on his team."

Jonesy Wilson lumbered up and plopped down next to
them. "Hey, fellow big shots."

"Well, hey to you, Mr. MVP." Dan reached over and
gave the big center another high five. "Way to cash in."

"Not a bad season." Jonesy looked from one to the other.
"Me and my dad figured that if I got on this team, we'd come
out on the right side of the river. And sure enough." He
fingered the medallion hanging around his neck.

"What'd you do with that big trophy?" Dan started to
laugh. "Your pop drives a truck, right? You're going to need
it to get that sucker home."

The three visited for a few more minutes before the
buzzer rang. "Well, I'll see you guys," Jonesy said, but he
didn't move to get up. There was an awkward moment as
he hesitated.

"Now what?" Dan never bothered with the social
graces. "If you want my autograph, just say so, Wilson."

"It ain't that." Jonesy scratched his head for a moment,
and then shrugged. "Shucks, I'll just tell you guys . . . man,
I really appreciated playing with you."

"Hey, our pleasure," Bucky said.

"No, not just that." The big center paused, thinking. "I
mean, you guys being Christians and everything. And always supporting everyone else on the team and stuff. And
praying all the time."

Bucky found himself almost holding his breath. Jonesy
was dead serious as he continued, "Well, I gotta tell you, it
kind of got to me. I mean, you guys hold this team together.
We could see it last year when I was with Walnut Creek,
and, man, over here too." He licked his lips, a bit nervous.
"And I just wanted you to know . . . it's . . . good." He gave

a little grin and then shrugged as if to let them know his tribute was finished.

Dan appeared about to say something, but abruptly stuck out his hand. The two athletes shook as Bucky watched and whispered to himself, "Thank You, Lord."

Jonesy stood up and began to leave, and then suddenly turned back. "You guys heard that Brayshaw called a base-ball meeting for this afternoon?"

"No." Bucky looked startled. "Season's not for several weeks."

"Yeah, I know." The tall center shook his head. "I don't play baseball, but I know you guys both go out for it."

"We should go to that," Bucky told Dan. "Maybe we'll get a handle on what kind of varsity schedule they're going to have." He looked up toward the sky as if to send up one more prayer.

As he walked through the murky corridors toward the other wing where his first afternoon class was, he suddenly saw Lisa in the hallway ahead of him. The unexpected encounter caused his pulse to race a bit. Should he call out to her? The two of them hadn't spoken since his ill-fated phone call from the beach of Waikiki the semester before. Her words from that moonlit evening—"*Bucky, leave me alone!*"—still rang in his ears. He slowed his walk, allowing her to get even farther down the hallway. She didn't look back as she went around the corner.

As he sat through the last class of the afternoon, his mind wandered back to the scene in the gymnasium. Championships were such fleeting things, he thought to himself. Sure, he and Dan had won "all the marbles," as Coach Brayshaw liked to say. But the minute one sport was over, another one immediately took center stage. By Wednesday morning the basketball medallions would be ancient history. He couldn't help wondering if the athletic director would be able to get him on the varsity baseball squad.

A knot of about 20 would-be baseball team members milled around outside the coach's office just after school let out. Bucky recognized a couple of the players from last year's frosh squad, who now had aspirations for JV or maybe even the coveted positions on varsity. Dan came ambling up from the other side. "What's going on?"

"Just got here myself."

Coach Brayshaw came in from the gym and looked over the group. "Have a seat," he told them, running his fingers through his hair. The students grabbed chairs or simply plopped themselves down on the thin carpeting.

"I guess . . . well, first of all, congratulations again to those of you who participated in our great basketball season." He paused. "Not just varsity either." He glanced at a couple of the players. "I know you JV players didn't win your division, but we had a great year, 9-7, and some of you are going to be terrific on the big team next fall. I mean that."

After a moment of silence he continued. Dan and Bucky glanced at each other, wondering what was behind his words.

"Anyway, I guess I better come right out and tell you why I called the meeting." Coach Brayshaw pulled a piece of paper out of his pocket and held it in his hand. "I got a fax this morning from a college back east. Some people I know back there from way back. And they've had a bit of, well, political messes, etc. Bottom line is, they've asked me to come back and take the position. Director of the whole program. Two of their men were here the other day to talk to me about it."

Bucky gulped, hardly believing what he was hearing. He remembered seeing the coach with some visitors in the gymnasium after the finals. That had to be them, he decided.

"You going to do it, Coach?" one of the JV players
blurted out.

The director hesitated. "Yeah, Ronny, I guess I am. I
mean, you men are a fine bunch. Outstanding, in fact." He
glanced in Bucky's general direction. "But to coach on the
college level is something I've always wanted to do—and
I'm never going to get a chance like this one again."

"Yeah, but what about baseball?" The same boy again.
"You're going now? Middle of the year?"

"I know this is abrupt," Brayshaw admitted. "But the
district has several names available right now—in fact, I
hear they've already got two men who can come here immediately, today."

Brayshaw continued, but Bucky found it hard to listen.
Brayshaw leaving? Halfway through their senior year, with
just one more possible athletic season? He thought back to
his freshman year and the traumatic altercation with the
hard-driving coach over playing in a game past Friday sundown. And then how God had worked to heal the relationship . . . and make Bucky one of the big guns in the
high school's athletic program. Time and time again,
Coach Brayshaw had publicly said that Dan Litton and
Bucky Stone were the catalyst for his teams. Now what was
going to happen?

He longed to tell the coach how much the three years
had meant to him, but this wasn't the time for that. The
other guys were still buzzing about the news and asking
questions. Finally he and Dan exited and began to walk toward the parking lot. "What do you think about that?" he
said at last.

Dan shook his head slowly. "Unbelievable."

CHAPTER 3

GEARING UP
FOR TRYOUTS

Traffic was a mess on Florentine Avenue as he drove
over to First California Bank, causing Bucky to be about
five minutes late. He shot Mr. Willis an apologetic look
and hurried to check in and get to his window. Already a
line of several customers stood waiting, and Bucky motioned to the first one standing in line.

During the past two years of working at the bank, the
young teller had mastered the art of being friendly while
still handling the customers' needs efficiently. Whenever
someone slowed things up by wanting to chat, Bucky was
good at giving the impression of wishing he could visit—
but of being "reluctantly obligated" to serve those still waiting in line. Customers invariably left his window feeling
complimented rather than annoyed. More than once Mr.
Willis had complimented Bucky on his good people skills.

Several times during the shift Bucky's mind returned to
the scene in the athletic department. How could Coach

Brayshaw leave right in the middle of the year? Despite the
ups and down of their early relationship, he realized now
what a genuine affection he felt for his coach.

Still, a question nagged at him. During the past three
years he'd never really carved out an opportunity to talk to
Brayshaw about being a Christian. Sure, Dan and Sam and
now Miss Cochran had made decisions for Jesus and been
baptized. But he'd never even cleared his throat to make
any such suggestion to his coach. Should he have done so?
He mulled over that question for some time, but drove
home sensing that if anyone at Hampton Beach High
School had a full understanding of Bucky's Christian faith,
it had to be the Panthers' athletic director.

The next Sabbath evening after supper at his house,
Bucky and Dan talked about the upcoming baseball season. Dan's father was away in Fresno for the weekend visiting an older sister, so the stocky ballplayer and Julie both
lingered later than usual. She sat on the couch next to him,
resting her head against his shoulder as the two guys discussed the upcoming baseball season.

"Look," Bucky asserted, "all we can do is be ready,
man. I mean 150 percent. We've got to drive ourselves so
hard that no matter who comes in, and no matter what
kind of schedule they throw at him, he'll have to use us."

"Yeah, but what can we do?" Dan looked over at Julie.
"We're already pushing full tilt. Running and all that." He
and Bucky were still putting in a full four miles just about
every morning.

"I don't know. Whatever we can do to practice baseball. Batting cages, whatever. It's just . . . man, this is our
last chance to be a witness in front of the whole school."

Julie sat up and straightened her hair. "Do baseball guys
train much before the season? I know they do in basketball."

"Not much," Dan admitted. "Do some throwing to

keep your arm in shape. That's about it."

"There you go, then," Bucky asserted. "Litton, we've got to let 'er rip these next two weeks. I mean, in basketball you were the one who whipped me into shape. We'd never have won those three titles if you hadn't pushed me."

"Yeah."

"I was even thinking of quitting at the bank," Bucky told him. "Just until the end of the year. So we could go all out."

His friend gulped at the suggestion. "You gonna do it?"

Bucky shook his head. "No, but I might cut back a little bit. Willis knows how bad you and I want to finish up the year with one more shot at the gold."

After a momentary silence Julie looked at both of them, her eyes serious. "I think it's so neat the way you guys both want to just play for, you know, honoring God. That's completely . . . different."

Dan looked at her soberly and then reached out and took her hand. "You're so lucky to have me for a boyfriend," he deadpanned. Bucky fell over on the rug, laughing.

⚾ ⚾ ⚾

And the next two weeks Bucky and Dan did indeed drive themselves harder than ever. Mr. Willis agreed to let Bucky trim his work schedule to just two afternoons a week during the baseball season, and the boys used the extra time to good advantage, working on their throwing and fielding.

"This guy at the gas station said he'd be glad to pitch to us Sunday afternoon," Dan told him after a long workout. "He played in college and still has a pretty good arm. Then I could catch while you hit, and you could do it for me."

"Man, that'd be great!" Then Bucky scowled. "Is he going to want to be paid or anything?"

"Are you kidding? The guy's a nut for baseball. He can't get enough of it, he tells me. If we just blow off some steam about how great he is, that'll be all the pay he needs."

Bucky's muscles ached the following Sunday evening after the long two-hour marathon of hitting, but he could feel a growing confidence. After last season with the junior team, it was a whole new challenge to face the hard sliders and curves that Ricardo had thrown at them, but the young athlete had a keen eye and good instincts in the batter's box. Hitting both right- and left-handed, he'd knocked plenty of the mechanic's pitches up against the distant fences. Plus he and Dan had wheedled the older player into two more sessions the coming Wednesday and Sunday.

"We're going to be ready," Dan told him the night before varsity tryouts. "As ready as it's possible to get, anyway." He and Julie sat across the library table from Bucky as they worked on a joint senior project for government class. "You watch, babe. Stone and me are going to pop a few long balls right across the freeway."

Skies were gray the next afternoon, but the threatened rain didn't seem to be coming as Coach Brayshaw gathered those trying out for baseball together on the field. Standing next to him was an older man with graying hair and a very tan complexion. "Guys, I want you to meet Coach Roger Demerest." A buzz of awkward greetings followed. "He comes to us from Idaho, and we're kind of lucky to get him right in the middle of the year this way. They had a big organizational shakeup up there, and our opening came along just in time. He's a real baseball man—in fact, we had a good time at lunch today trading stories." Brayshaw turned to directly face his replacement. "These are good athletes we're giving you, Coach Demerest, and I'll be real disappointed if you don't drive them hard right into the winner's circle. No kidding." He added the last with a bit of forced joviality.

After a few quick introductions, the new man efficiently

organized tryouts, using his two assistant trainers to help su-
pervise the hitting, fielding, and baserunning competitions. A
few minutes later, Brayshaw wisely departed from the field,
giving the replacement director a free hand. Bucky glanced
over from the batting cages and watched as his mentor of
three years put a box of things in the trunk of his car.

"Just a sec," he said to Ron, who was coordinating the hitters. "I'll be right back." He and Dan trotted over to the parking lot just as Brayshaw was getting into the driver's seat.

"Are we going to see you again?" Bucky asked.

A tight pause. "Flight's tomorrow afternoon. Cindy
and I gotta head out pretty early in the morning." He
squinted, looking over at the field swarming with high
school ballplayers.

Bucky put out his hand and the coach shook it. "Thanks
for everything. You were a great coach, and Dan and I
really liked playing for you."

"For sure," Dan added, shaking hands with Brayshaw.
"You were the greatest. Coach of the year, I tried to keep
telling you."

The athletic director managed a chuckle, then grew
sober. "Well, you two men were very special," he said at
last. "Not just because you brought this school all those
championships, but . . ." His voice trailed off.

Bucky waited. Was this the opportunity he'd wanted?

But the moment passed. "You guys brought the team together," Brayshaw told them. "And I knew I could count on
you. So—thanks. I mean, for everything." It seemed like he
wanted to say something else, that some hidden reserved
thought, some reaction to their faith in Jesus Christ needed
to be mentioned. But it just wasn't going to come out. Not
today. Dan and Bucky glanced at each other, and then
kind of edged away. They stood in the parking lot and
waved as the older man's sedan turned the corner.

"He's a good guy," Dan managed, his voice unusually subdued.

They walked slowly back over to the batting cage, the grass crunching under Bucky's feet. Should he have said something to Coach Brayshaw about his faith in God? He hadn't felt any kind of indication that he should speak—but was that a good guide?

Dan broke the reverie. "Time to hit a few smokers, Buck. I mean, right this minute."

"You're up next, Stone," the new coach motioned, matching athletes' jersey numbers with a list he had on his clipboard. Bucky whispered a silent prayer as he donned a batting helmet and picked up his favorite bat. He and Dan had just been through an extensive hitting workout the evening before, so he felt as ready as he had ever been in his life. Still, it was a different pitcher out there on the mound. Everyone knew Dennis was the school's varsity ace.

"Go easy on me!" he hollered out to the hurler, waving his bat back and forth and taking a deep breath. He tried to grin, but he could feel the tension.

The first pitch came slicing in hard, but it was clearly outside. Bucky let it go by and saw the coach nodding. "Good eye."

The next one was closer to the plate but still outside. Not wanting to have a reputation as a looker, Bucky slapped at the ball and poked a hard single through the right side of the infield. "Nice one!" Coach Demerest said. "Way to go with the pitch."

For the next five minutes, Bucky rocketed shot after shot deep into the outfield. His timing on offspeed pitches was nearly perfect, and on two of Dennis's hard fastballs he smashed balls over the fence. He was glowing as he finally stepped out and tossed his batting helmet against the backstop. Out of the corner of his eye he could see the new athletic director nod at the assistant trainer and write something down on his chart.

"Lord, You did it!" he whispered, almost aloud, still feeling pumped up from knowing he'd had a hot session. "Help Dan too!"

A couple minutes later the pitcher walked off the mound and approached home plate with a huge grin on his face. "Come on," he complained with a laugh. "I can't get nothin' past these two guys. Let someone else pitch." Dan had sprayed vicious line drives all over the outfield, bashing a number of deep drives up against the fence. Only two pitches so far had rolled into fielders' gloves or been caught in the outfield.

"Just remember, they'll be playing for us," Coach Demerest retorted. "It's your job to get the other team's batters out, not our guys." He paused. "You sure you're giving them your best stuff? They didn't promise you a free Big Mac or something?"

"No way, man," the catcher piped up from his position behind the plate. "That was Ace Ventura heat comin' in, Coach. These guys are just hot, that's all."

Defensive practice was equally a showcase for the Litton/Stone team as the two outfielders alertly picked off fly balls and wicked line drives. Ricardo's three training sessions with them had paid off handsomely, as Bucky and Dan demonstrated their range and accurately hit the cutoff man with balls batted up against the fence. Dan in particular drew gasps as he successfully dove for a "gapper" that would otherwise have been a sure triple.

Bucky was still tingling as the players showered off after the practice session. "Man, that was almost . . . like Twilight Zone or something," he muttered to his teammate as he washed away the grime from the playing field. "I couldn't get that many hits in five years of playing."

"I know. And three homers off our best pitcher." .

"Guess all we do now is wait. What's-his-name said he isn't going to post the varsity list until Monday."

As the two were dressing, Ron poked his head into the still steamy dressing area. "Litton? Stone? Can you guys spare a couple minutes? Coach Demerest would like to see you."

Bucky gulped. What could it be about? He knew the practice session had gone well.

The new athletic director was more formal than Bray-shaw had been. Instead of the familiar feet-propped-up-on-the-desk, he sat squarely behind it with a stoic expression on his face. "You're Stone, right? And Litton?" He offered them each a firm handshake, then motioned to the two chairs. "Have a seat, men."

Dan glanced over at his teammate as they sat down. "What's . . . up?" He coughed nervously.

Coach Demerest picked up his clipboard and glanced through the numbers. "Well, obviously, you two men are decent ballplayers." For the first time, he showed the trace of a smile. "In fact, you're a bit more than decent, actually." He glanced from one to the other. "That was about the best hitting I've seen in a few years, and you were whacking them off one of the better arms in the district."

Bucky grinned. "Thanks, Coach. I guess we just kind of got in a zone or something."

The older man shook his head. "I don't think so. From what Brayshaw tells me in this long report he left behind, you two men are the best in the school, period. Basketball and baseball."

The younger player could feel his face flushing. All the extra hours of practice, the hard driving, the drills with Dan, were about to pay off, it seemed. He gave his team-mate a bit of a thumbs-up gesture.

Coach Demerest pushed back his chair a bit and

crossed his legs, assuming a less formal position. "Now, then," he continued, picking up a pencil and examining its point. "What's this here about Friday games? Your former coach says you can't play."

A long silence. Several times already Bucky had had to make this exact same speech about his Adventist faith and how sundown-to-sundown belonged to God. Surprisingly, though, it was Dan who spoke first. "That's right, Coach. Stone and I are Seventh-day Adventists, and we can't play games on Friday nights or on Saturdays."

"Well, Saturday's no problem," the older man said easily. "District never has games then."

"I know, but Friday evenings after sundown—we can't play then either," Dan asserted.

Demerest pulled his chair closer and looked hard at first one, then the other. "Wait a minute. You can't play *ever* on a Friday night? Not a single time?"

Dan shook his head, and glanced over at his teammate for support. Bucky felt a flash of pride at his friend's courage. "Coach, that's our Sabbath," he interjected. "Friday evening and Saturday. We don't work that day, and we don't participate in school sports. Nothing like that."

"Well, sure," the older man responded. "Fine. That's your usual practice for . . . you know, regular. Someone wants to keep something like that, I'm all for it. Religion's a good thing. And a guy tries to arrange his schedule to do whatever he feels like doing. But when it comes to a game, to a team event where we count on each other—you can't do it then. A team's got to have its players, and we have to sacrifice a little bit."

The coach's words seemed to echo in the room. "Well, we want to do all we can to help the team," Bucky told him. "I mean, Litton and I are both seniors. We for sure want the Panthers to win this year—it's our last chance." He drew another breath. "But we can't play on our Sabbath."

"No matter *what?*" Now the coach was getting a bit red in the face. "I mean, what about playoff games? Suppose you get into the blessed world series. And it just happens to be on a Friday night. The two of you are going to go to church instead, after you and your teammates have driven all the way down to the end zone like that?"

The oddly mixed metaphor hung in the air between the three men. "How . . . how many games are there on Friday night this year?" Bucky asked, his voice suddenly timid.

The older man glanced across his desk and ran his finger down the list. "Well, actually looks like only two," he admitted. "But that's in the regular season. Varsity playoff schedule this year is squeezed up, more like basketball's been. I'm almost positive it's going to be a Monday-Wednesday-Friday round."

Bucky's mind raced back through the past three years of athletic turmoil at Hampton Beach High School. To the Friday night where he *had* played in a game that went past sundown . . . and the sick feeling in his heart as he trudged home, followed by a renewed determination never to do it again. He could still hear the angry shouts of Coach Brayshaw ordering him off the playing field right in the middle of the Panthers' most crucial contest. Then the aborted season after he broke his arm, and the year he and Dan had endured as juniors playing on the lowly frosh team. Was their entire high school baseball experience going to end prematurely right here in this cramped office?

Deep in thought, Dan suddenly cleared his throat. "Couple of times, Brayshaw was able to get games moved for us," he told the coach. "At least in basketball."

Demerest's face tightened. "Yeah, I heard about that," he retorted, "and I heard how he got screamed at by district over it. Stevens told him, 'No way ever again.' Did you know that?" With a bit of scorn in his voice he added, "Look, I'm going to level with you boys. I don't do business that way. A team's a team, and a player who's not willing to give a bit for the good of the team . . . well, I haven't got much use for that kind of attitude." He looked from Dan to Bucky, daring them to challenge him.

Bucky half-rose out of his chair and slowly picked up his duffel bag. "Coach," he said simply, "Dan and I want to play. We've worked our tails off these past few weeks to be ready to play varsity. If you play us, we'll give a million percent every game, every play, every practice, every ev-erything. We won't let you down. Ever." He gulped, trying to force down the knot in his throat. "But we won't go against our consciences."

CHAPTER 4

BACK ON
THE BENCH

A raw, almost vicious rain swept through the Bay Area that Friday night. It pounded down hard on the roof just outside Bucky's second-story window as he sat at his desk staring out at the gale. For this time of March, such an intense storm felt almost hostile—in fact, a few jagged bursts of lightning seemed to be deliberately attacking the distant coastline.

"Somebody must be mad at us," he muttered to himself, going over to the door and flipping off the light switch. Now the rain and the roar of the wind seemed even more cruel as the tree limbs outside his window shuddered in near-surrender. The recent interview with Coach Demerest was an unreal memory in such sopping weather, but Bucky knew that the confrontation still remained unresolved. Brayshaw would have jumped through hoops to get those Friday evening games moved, but the new man seemed to have a completely different attitude. The tall athlete gazed out at the turmoil, remembering an Old Testament verse from one of Pastor Jensen's sermons about a new pharaoh coming along in Egypt who "knew not Joseph."

It was late now, and the rest of the family had gone to bed already. Dad was away again on one of his professional skills upgrade trips, and both Mom and Rachel Marie had called it a night back around 9:30. But somehow the fierceness of the storm fascinated Bucky—he didn't feel sleepy at all.

What about Lisa?

He kicked against the wall in disgust as the stray thought popped into his mind for the hundredth time in the past month. It was so stupid to keep thinking about her all the time! "Things are totally, totally, *totally* over with her, you moron," he grumbled to himself. It was stupid to have your mind play such broken-record tricks.

But it seemed as if he spotted the senior girl at school just often enough to keep his emotions from dying. Every time he passed her in the hallway at school, the old feelings would come surging back. And just last week, during a bit of a drizzle, he'd spotted her crossing the street as he'd pulled out into traffic in his little Toyota. For a moment he'd almost honked, but held back at the last minute.

Another quick flash of lightning and a low rumble in the distance. Thunder was unusual in the Bay Area, and Bucky reached out to make sure the window was all the way closed. He flopped down on the bed.

Almost a whole quarter had gone by now since his ill-fated phone call to Lisa. Her words had stuck in his mind with a painful ache: "*Bucky, leave me alone!*"

But he didn't want to leave her alone! Three and a half years after that first awkward meeting when he'd seen a pretty freshman girl at registration, she was still the one he wanted. So something was wrong—why couldn't he fix it? Maybe she was mad at him—then he could find out why. He wasn't a little kid who had to spend the rest of his life missing out on something special without knowing the reason for it.

Maybe he could call her about something innocent . . . and then pick up some clue. *"Uh, do you know the capital of Connecticut? I need it for a history paper."* Something like that. He rejected the idea immediately—it was that kind of brilliant impulse that had gotten him in trouble calling her from Waikiki.

Monday morning between classes one of the student assistants from the athletic department tracked him down. "Coach Demerest wanted to see you," she informed him. "Litton too."

Something lurched in his guts. "Be right there."

It took a few minutes to find his teammate, and they hurried over to the athletic complex. It would make them both late for their next class, they knew. But they had to know what Demerest wanted.

"Sit down." The gray-haired coach didn't waste any time. "We may as well get this stuff settled right now." He looked from one boy to the other. "I've got to post my varsity list today, and I may as well tell you, the two of you'd be my top names."

Bucky felt a warm glow start around his neck and cause a blush. "Wow. Thanks, Coach."

"Well, now just hang on." Demerest shifted in his seat. "That all has to do with what you men decide right now about these Friday games."

"What . . . what about them?"

"Are you going to play?" Coach shot out the challenge. "We've got two on Friday nights, one here and one over in Concord. Big games, both of 'em. They could make or break the schedule for us. And I've got to know if I can have you in my lineup."

Bucky hesitated just a moment before he spoke. "Well, Coach, you know we want to play. Both of us. But we can't play in those two games if they go past sundown."

"Well, of course they go past sundown," he retorted. "They start at 7:00 in the evening. It's a night game, Stone. Give me a break."

"I guess we can't play then," Bucky said evenly. "Not on Friday night."

"And that's it? You don't want to think about it? Nothing?"

Dan cleared his throat. "Coach, we've been thinking about it for three years already. These are our beliefs. We're not going to ditch them now."

For a tense moment the new coach silently looked from one to the other. "You're serious, aren't you?" He didn't say it with any admiration.

Bucky sucked in his breath. "Look," he managed. "Dan and I are Christians. The reason we play as hard as we do is *because* we're Christians. It's what . . . makes us work. And so far we've won a JV title and two varsity championships because of it."

"All by yourselves? Just you two boys and your Bibles?" Sarcasm hung thick in the older man's voice.

Bucky blushed. He hadn't meant to make it sound like that. "No, of course not," he managed. "But as far as *us* doing our best, it's our faith in God that makes us that way. And I think we at least had a part in helping those teams win." He added the last bit defensively.

The man mumbled something inaudible to himself as he reflected on the impasse. Bucky wondered exactly what Coach Brayshaw had told him about their unique situation.

At last the man looked up with a heavy sigh. "Well, I'm in a mess," he told them. "You two are the best athletes in the school. And, I mean, that tryout was an open-and-shut case. You guys slam-dunked it—no two ways about it." He tapped a pencil angrily on the desk, still thinking hard.

"Are we on the team?" Now Dan was a bit impatient himself.

"Yeah, Litton, you are. Both of you are." The coach returned his gaze. "But you're both gonna be back-up players because of this. And that's a stinking shame that I can't put the two best hitters in the school in my starting lineup. But I have to play people who will guarantee to show up at all 20 games."

"So where does that leave us?" Bucky asked.

"Leaves you playing when I tell you. Pinch-hitting once in a while. You fill in during the late innings if it's close. Somebody gets sick, and I let you play. Like that." He scribbled a doodle on the paper in front of him. "You change your mind, though, and I'll let you bat three and four right through to the end of the World Series."

He cocked an eyebrow, waiting. "So what's it going to be?"

Bucky stood up, his face still flushed. "I guess we're your subs then."

Dan stood too, with a retort trembling on his lips. But he held back and followed his friend out the door.

"So now what?" Dan paced angrily back and forth by the football bleachers. They had decided that with the class period already halfway finished, they might as well skip it. "What a turkey! Man, how can we get Brayshaw back?"

"He's just doing what he thinks is best for the team."

"Keeping us off just because of two games?"

Bucky glanced back at the PE complex. "Well, look, every coach wants to be able to play the same starting nine whenever he can."

Dan sat down heavily. "We ought to just quit." He kicked at a dirt clod in disgust.

"No way." The younger boy leaned against a bleacher and looked at his friend. "We're not quittin', Litton."

"Why not? You want to ride the bench all season?"

"'Course not. But look. You and I are going to train harder than anybody, push harder than anybody, help the other guys on the team harder than anybody. Then when there's an opening, or we pinch-hit for someone, or someone gets run over by a car, then we'll be ready." He managed a grin. "So grab your car keys and let's do some running over."

Dan drummed his fingers on the metal seat, then gave it a little *pop!* "I guess that's how you did finally get on the starting five on JV back when we were sophomores," he admitted.

In the distance they could hear the buzzer announcing the end of the period. "I guess that's us," Bucky told his friend.

Dan sighed heavily. "I guess we should have figured it wouldn't be any easier than this. At least we're on the team. Now we let God open up whatever He wants to open up."

"Uh huh." Despite his own frustration, Bucky marveled at Dan's spiritual insights. God was really working in the life of his teammate.

As they approached the ad building, he suddenly remembered something. "Litton, are we going to that concert next Saturday night like we talked about?"

"You mean 'Glad'?"

"Yeah, those guys."

"You find out about tickets?"

"I called the Christian bookstore, and they said $9.50 each."

"Sam for sure wants to go too?"

"Yup. He gets in Thursday from PUC. Said if we could get tickets to count him in."

Dan shivered in the cold March wind. "Let's go."

Bucky hesitated. "Shall I get four tickets so Julie can go too?"

"Do you guys mind?"

"I don't." His friend laughed. "I figure I owe you one after that Hawaii mess anyway, where I stiffed you about three times in a row."

"That's true, shorty." Dan gave Bucky a friendly kick in the shins. "OK. Four tickets. You get 'em, and I'll pay you back. I don't mind driving. It's just up to Sacramento, right?"

"Yeah. Calvary Church."

"That's the big one right off the freeway, right?"

"Uh huh." The two broke into a jog just as the second bell rang. "Ack. We're late."

That evening after his work period at First California Bank, Bucky waited until Mom and Rachel Marie had left for their weekly grocery trip before plopping down next to the kitchen phone. He had the whole house to himself in case his plan didn't work.

"First off, I ask her if she has a copy of the Constitution," he told himself. He could have brought one home from school, but he'd accidentally-on-purpose left it behind so he'd have an excuse to call. Even Lisa couldn't get mad at him for legitimately needing something for government class. Then, if Part One went well, he could at least mention the Glad concert in Sacramento. That was for sure a low-percentage option, but if for some reason it sounded like the old Lisa had miraculously returned—well, he'd play it by ear.

". . . I'm sorry, the number you have dialed is no longer in service." *What?* Punching in the seven digits a second time, he got the same bored recording. He knew the senior girl hadn't moved away from Hampton Beach. Just that afternoon he had seen her out in the parking lot talking to some teacher he didn't know. Scowling in frustration, he set the receiver back in place.

"I swear she ain't worth it," he muttered to himself as he went upstairs and gave his books an angry toss onto the bed. The less-than-ideal varsity situation and his eternally unsuccessful quest for Lisa were turning into twin aggravations during what was supposed to be such a triumphant senior year.

At the Friday night concert, though, some of his resentment began to burn away. The smooth, inventive harmonies of Glad were even better than on his full collection of their CDs. Calvary Church had set up a huge sound system to rival any Bay Area rock concert, and the five singers were at the top of their form, performing crowd favorites from their a cappella and contemporary albums.

"These guys are awesome!" Sam whistled his approval as the quintet finished yet another medley. "It sounds like 15 guys singing up there."

"Well, they dub in the extra voices off their music tracks so they get the full range," Bucky told him, leaning over past Dan and Julie. "I read about it in the paper yesterday."

Julie gave her boyfriend a nudge. "That one on the end's sure cute. Don't you think?" A mischievous grin curled around her mouth.

Dan shrugged, refusing to take the bait. "Nah. He can't weigh more than about 140. I could sit on him easy."

"He can sure sing, though." Bucky was savoring every note of the concert. So far they had sung every hit he'd driven to Sacramento to hear.

Suddenly he sucked in his breath. The group had just started singing another song, but he leaned over and whispered in Dan's ear anyway. "Litton, who's that up there?"

"Where?" Dan cocked his head.

"Right up there. Second row."

"Nobody I know."

Bucky edged out a few inches into the aisle of the crowded sanctuary. Seated right near the front, a tall young man had his eyes closed and hands raised in the air as Glad did a slow rendition of "I'm Forever Grateful." "Man, I know that guy," Bucky muttered to himself.

On the chorus of the familiar gospel song, the entire audience sang with the group members. Standing in the aisle now, right by the huge speakers, the same person had his hands clasped in front of him. From where Bucky was standing, he couldn't quite make out his profile.

The last haunting notes faded away, and a kind of reverent applause filled the church as it faded into darkness. A single spotlight from the balcony illuminated a large cross suspended from the ceiling over the singers. "That was great," Julie murmured, nestling her head against Dan's shoulder. "Thanks for bringing me, babe."

Just then Bucky watched in fascination as the same young man walked onto the platform and embraced Ed Nalle, Glad's lead singer. He then picked up a microphone. "What a night!" he exclaimed, emotion filling his voice. "Jesus has been here tonight. Amen?" The applause swelled.

All at once goosebumps struck Bucky from head to toe. He gave a little gasp and clutched at Dan's arm. "Litton, do you know who that is?"

His friend pulled away, giving his friend an odd look. "What are you getting so excited about, Stone? Who?"

Bucky could hardly get the words out. "That guy up front. That's Hilliard! Jeff Hilliard!"

"Huh?" The name didn't register with Dan.

"Hilliard! He hated us! That baseball pitcher who popped me on the arm two years ago! That's him up front right there!"

CHAPTER 5

FORGIVING
YOUR ENEMY

The huge crowd was streaming toward the exits, so it was hard to thread their way toward the platform. "Excuse me," Bucky said over and over, trying to keep his eyes on the student who was now visiting with some of the stage hands already tearing down the PA equipment.

"You sure that's him?" Dan and Julie, still holding hands, were right behind him.

"It's gotta be." The ballfield incident from two years ago was still fresh in his mind. Many times since then he'd relived both the anger and pain as the disgruntled pitcher's fastball had whistled through the air and broken his left arm right at the elbow.

The members of the singing group had exited now through a side door, and most of those lingering near the platform eagerly followed after them. Splitting away from his threesome, Bucky approached the tall young man, his heart in his throat. "Excuse me," he managed, trying to keep his pulse from racing.

The stranger set down a microphone and turned toward him. "Yeah. What's up?"

Bucky licked his lips. "I, uh . . . I don't know if you remember me," he began.

The other student looked older than Bucky, maybe 18 or even closer to 19. "Whoa," he said. "You do look familiar. But I . . ." His voice trailed away as he squinted through the dimmed sanctuary lighting. At last he shook his head. "I'm sorry, man. I guess I don't remember. Do you go to Calvary here?" He seemed genuinely puzzled.

A shake of the head. "No, I . . . we drove up from Hampton Beach."

All at once a startled expression came over the other student's face. "Wait," he breathed, his voice tense. "Hang on. You're . . . Stone. Man, you're Bucky Stone."

"Yeah." All at once Bucky's mind went blank, and he couldn't think of anything else to say.

Jeff gulped. "Man! Stone, it's you! This is unbelievable!"

Bucky's mind was still a blank. "I guess we were kind of surprised to see you again," he managed at last.

"*You* were surprised! Are you kidding? Ever since I came to the Lord three months ago, He's been hittin' me over the head about you. 'You've got to go talk to Stone!' But I hadn't done it yet." The words came out in short animated bursts.

"What do you mean?"

Jeff's voice suddenly became sober. "Two years ago I hit you with that fastball. Out there on the ballfield." He brushed at the corner of one eye. "It was a wrong thing to do, Stone. I've got to ask for your forgiveness. Like right now."

His statement took Bucky by surprise. "I . . . uh . . ."

Hilliard, who topped Bucky by a full two inches, stepped closer. "Please. Stone, you've got to forgive me. I mean, I gave my heart to the Lord and I'm a member here and everything, but what I did to you . . ." His eyes searched the younger boy's face.

Bucky could feel his heart pounding with excitement. "Well, sure!" He glanced over at Dan. "I forgive you, man. Absolutely!" The two stood there staring at each other on the murky stage, tangled PA cords strewn around their feet. All at once they were embracing, pounding each other on the back over and over.

"Oh, boys . . ." Despite the magic of the moment, Dan had to get in a word. "Remember us?"

Bucky managed a laugh as the two athletes separated at last. "I'm sorry," he apologized. "Jeff, you remember Dan Litton."

"Boy, I sure do." Jeff offered a handshake. "Man, you were about the best power hitter at Hampton."

"Still is," Bucky put in. "And this is Sam, and here's Julie. She's kind of attached to Mr. Litton at the moment."

"That's great." Jeff Hilliard's newfound faith seemed to jump out of every pore. "I can't believe this. It's great to see you guys."

"So how'd you become a Christian?" Dan didn't waste any time asking.

"Right here." Jeff made a motion toward the rest of the sanctuary. "'Bout three months ago some guys from here invited my girlfriend and me to come to a concert. And that same night I guess the Holy Spirit just grabbed onto me. Said, 'Hilliard, you've fooled around long enough. Tonight's the night.'" He glanced at the four students. "How about you guys?" He scratched at his mustache, thinking. "Stone, you were kind of with that Adventist group, weren't you?" He reddened a bit. "I guess that's how things kind of went bad at first. Me ragging on you for that Friday night stuff."

Bucky nodded. "Yeah. And Dan and Sam are both Adventists now too."

"Huh." Jeff looked startled. "That's great." He looked over at Julie. "How about you?"

She laughed easily. "Oh, I'm just taking it all in."

An older man with a full beard came over. "Hilliard, we're about done here. You can go with your friends if you want. Bailey and I can finish up."

Jeff nodded. "Do you guys want to go out or something? Man, we've got a lot to talk about."

"We were going to get a late snack before driving home," Bucky told him. "Why don't you join us?" He hesitated. "Is your girlfriend here?"

Hilliard winced just a bit. "No. We kind of broke up right after I joined the church here. She's not a believer."

"That's too bad." Bucky shot Dan a quick glance. "OK with you, Litton? Can Jeff come along with us?"

"Sure." Dan pulled out the keys to his Camaro. "I hope you have your own car, though, Hilliard. Your legs aren't going to fit anywhere in mine."

For the next hour and a half they sat around two tables pushed together at a nearby Wendy's. Obviously relieved to have the broken-arm incident disposed of, Jeff chattered on happily about his new job at Calvary Church with the special events team and the teen division.

"Do you still play ball?" Dan wanted to know.

A big nod as Jeff took another big bite out of his hamburger. "Yeah."

"I thought you were a year ahead of us," Bucky interjected.

"Huh uh. I was a sophomore too, back when . . . you know. Same as you guys."

"But you'd already been on varsity? Your freshman year?"

Jeff hesitated. "Yeah, just right at the end. Coach

What's-his-name said I had a good fastball . . ."

"Brayshaw?"

"Yeah. And he gave me a shot. But I walked a bunch of guys. I'd get them one-and-two and then lose them. And then the next year when I blew it and threw at you . . . I was out the whole year. My mom had to move the next year, and so I ended up at Dixon."

"Wait a minute!" Dan set down his drink. "That's still in our district!"

"Yeah. I think we're on the very border of the conference. From there on north, it's Sacramento."

"So are you playing this year?" Sam asked.

"Yeah. I'm on their varsity squad." Suddenly his eyes had a gleam to them. "I guess maybe that means we might end up playing each other."

Bucky burst into laughter. "And if we do, man, you owe me one clean fastball right down the middle of the plate." He poked a finger toward the other student's face. "I'll take it in the bottom of the seventh, bases loaded, if you don't mind."

"Man, that'd be heavy." The mood quieted down. "Going up against a fellow Christian for the championship." He glanced from Bucky over to Dan. "Boy, you never can tell. Dixon's got a pretty good team this year too. How about you guys?"

Dan grinned. "I don't care how born-again you are, Hilliard. Stone and me are going to stomp all over you on our way to the title."

"And give God the glory while you're doing it." Jeff reached out and offered Dan a high five. "Matthew 5:16 and all of that."

The familiar verse gave Bucky another dose of goose bumps. Could this really be hard-throwing Jeff Hilliard sitting with them talking about the Lord and quoting the Bible? Unbelievable!

⚾ ⚾ ⚾

Traffic was light on Interstate 80 as the four students drove south to Hampton Beach. Dan had the stereo on low, but the music didn't interrupt the spiritual glow that still lingered after the visit at the restaurant.

"Who'd have thunk it?" Still holding hands with Julie across the bucket seats in the front, Dan jockeyed around to glance back at Bucky. "Old Hilliard the Assassin gets converted." He changed lanes and gave a shake of his head. "Stone, you think he'll come down and visit our church?"

"He said he would." Bucky was still tingling from the encounter. He'd actually forgotten the beanball incident from his sophomore year until tonight, but it felt marvelous to have the matter forgiven—with him as the *forgiver*. And to know Jeff was a Christian now was easily as exciting as when Miss Cochran had been baptized a year ago. "I kind of wish we had a big 2,000-member superchurch like Calvary, though. Hilliard's going to think we're small potatoes."

"Nah." Dan shrugged. "Not with cool guys like us three. And a babe like Julie here. I'm going to baptize her myself before graduation." He reached up and pushed the top of her head under an imaginary pool of water.

Bucky looked past Sam and out the rear passenger window at the traffic going by on the other side of the freeway. Why were Christian churches so divided? He loved the special truths of the Adventist faith—the Sabbath and the certainty of Jesus' soon coming. But it was great to visit a huge church like Calvary, with its contemporary musical groups and social groups. And Jeff had clearly had an encounter with Jesus—nobody could deny that. Did the Seventh-day Adventist denomination really have something new to offer to a high school senior who already loved God with such intensity?

CHAPTER 6

HOME RUN HERO

The smells of cotton candy mingled with the odor of cattle manure as Bucky and Rachel Marie twisted their way through the crowds at the fair. "Are we almost there?" she wanted to know.

"Yeah, almost." The huge ferris wheel was just up ahead, and he fingered the last ride coupons in the pocket of his jeans.

Carnival rides and the sucker games at a fair weren't his thing at all—and he hated to give up a whole Sunday afternoon. But Bucky knew that there wouldn't be very many more Sundays to spend with his sister. Next school year he'd be away at PUC, and things would never be the same again. Sometimes you had to just put away your school books and your varsity baseball schedule, and give yourself to your higher commitments. Even though he didn't always feel like it, Rachel Marie was that important to him. In a way, it was kind of like keeping the Sabbath. You set everything else aside just because you knew in your heart it was the right thing.

It was a slow-moving ferris wheel, but the little swoop right at the top still made his stomach jump a little bit. Rachel Marie giggled with every revolution of the giant wheel, pointing to the odd sights below as the breeze tugged at her loose strands of hair. "This is fun!"

A pang of loneliness suddenly tugged at him, and he quietly slipped his arm around her. "Yeah, it is." He gave her a squeeze. "I'm glad you're having fun, kid."

He and Dad sat up late that evening, watching a rerun of *Pride of the Yankees,* the old black-and-white baseball movie about Lou Gehrig. It was almost midnight when the picture disappeared into a tiny dot in the center of the screen. "He was quite a player," Dad observed, scowling at his watch. "Better than you and Litton are ever going to be if you stay up like this ever again. Don't tell your coach it was my idea." He gave his son an affectionate swat on the rear as Bucky headed upstairs.

Baseball practices the next week were intense affairs, with the new coach pushing everyone to get ready for Game One. Bucky and Dan, determined to put their disappointment behind them, trained hard and also fired up the other players with their enthusiasm. "Go, baby! Whack that ball!" Dan screamed from the dugout at Erick, a junior with plenty of power. The batter obliged with a base hit right up the middle. "All right!" Bucky joined his teammate on the dugout steps. "Good poke!" Dan yelled.

"Think we'll get into games much?" Bucky unlaced his cleats and tossed them into his duffel bag after practice.

"Some. You keep hitting line-drive doubles in B.P. and Demerest won't have much choice."

Bucky grinned. "Boy, when that one new guy pitches,

you can always tell what's coming. He really tips off his off-speed stuff."

"I think you hurt his feelings," Dan told him, peeling off his undershirt. He paused, leaning against the faded green lockers. "You ever think about, you know, talking to Lisa anymore? Julie and I saw her at the mall last night."

Startled at the abrupt switch in topics, Bucky glanced up at him. He'd just been thinking about the senior girl the evening before. But he shook his head. "Naw. No more for me, Litton. Next year."

That evening, though, as he finished up a science paper up in his bedroom, his mind returned to the unresolved question of Miss Lisa Nichols. What was happening with her? Was she OK?

Feeling his face redden, he reached into the bottom drawer of his desk and dug out an old picture from their freshman year. He was embarrassed about having it—in fact, none of his family knew the photo was still in the house. For a long moment, he looked at it, remembering. As he glanced at the romantic little message she'd penned on the back, an emotion tugged at him as he saw the familiar handwriting.

He realized with a start that something inside of him was beginning to care more about *her* than about *romance* with her. It was a thought he'd never considered before. Could God use him to be a blessing to her . . . especially if he was willing to "let her go"?

Although he tried to express that in his prayer, it was hard to articulate. "I think You know what I mean, Lord," he muttered at last. "Well, I guess You *do* know what I mean—I'm just not sure myself what I mean. But if You can make me willing to give Lisa up to You as far as romance is concerned, then please use me to help her if she needs it." He added a few words in his prayer for Jonesy Wilson, the big basketball center, and also for Jeff Hilliard.

Thursday between classes he and Dan got wound up in a baseball discussion between classes, causing them both to be late to government class. "Whooh! Teacher ain't here yet," Dan grunted in relief, noticing the empty desk at the front of the half-filled classroom. "We got away with one, Stone."

Several minutes went by before they heard someone at the door. Miss Pendleton, a stocky woman from the registrar's office, walked in with an uncertain look on her face. "This is government, isn't it?"

"Yeah." Several seniors answered at once.

"I'm afraid we have bad news. Mrs. Randall has had a medical emergency come up, and we just found out she's going to be out for an extended time. Maybe even the rest of the year."

A buzz of sympathetic interest spread through the room. Bucky glanced over at his best friend, cocking an eyebrow.

"In a way, we're fortunate that this isn't a very full class. And there's another section of it being offered at the same time. Mr. Salomon says we're going to have to just merge the two together. They're down in B142, which is around the corner."

A girl behind Bucky raised her hand. "Are they at the same place in the book and all of that?"

"I don't know. Mr. Rojas will have to handle that. I'm sure he'll make allowances for whatever curriculum you were doing."

"When do we go?" Dan boomed out the question.

"Right now." The woman glanced up at the hall clock. "They're expecting you."

The 15 or so students clattered noisily down the empty hallway toward the other class section. Bucky hadn't really connected with Mrs. Randall, but he still felt a twinge of sympathy. He made a mental note that he and Dan should get her a get-well card or something. Maybe the front office would have more details after school.

Mr. Rojas, a dynamic instructor with a PE teacher's muscular build, motioned the visitors into his room. "You'll all have to stand against the wall all semester until graduation," he teased. "We don't have any room for you turkeys."

If anything, this section was even less full than Mrs. Randall's had been. As Bucky surveyed the half-empty classroom, his eyes suddenly landed on a familiar figure in the far corner. Seated alone, Lisa was bent over a drawing, idly sketching something. He gulped and sat down next to Dan in the second row, his pulse racing.

"Yeah, I saw her too," Dan leaned over and murmured in a low voice, trying not to laugh as he noticed his friend's discomfort.

⚾ ⚾ ⚾

Monday afternoon Bucky pulled a muted gray Panthers jersey on and carefully tucked it in. A nervous rumble of optimism filled the visitors' locker room. Coach Demerest had pulled together a good team, but the switch in coaches had been a jarring experience, and no one at Hampton Beach was about to predict what kind of season it was going to be.

Just as Dan was tying his shoelaces, the new athletic director came around the corner and headed right for him, clipboard in hand. "Litton, you're in right," he told him, his face all business. "Crook is out with some kind of bug, they say."

It was one of those situations where you couldn't look either too happy or sad. "Oh," Dan said, startled by the news. "OK, Coach."

"All right!" Bucky hissed at him as soon as Demerest had

left. "Our prayers have been answered—Crook got sick!"

"*You're* sick." Dan managed a grin. "Wish me luck, shorty."

Coach Demerest hadn't adjusted the batting lineup, so Dan batted in the right fielder's number 6 position. Pitching was ragged on both sides, and by the time they got to the sixth inning, the muscular replacement player had already gone a cool three-for-four at the plate, with three runs batted in all by himself. "Let's get some more," Bucky exhorted, clapping as the Panthers came trooping in from the field after the third out. "Two-run lead ain't enough."

The visitors were retired in order, and the home team, taking advantage of a pair of walks, bunted both runners into scoring position, where they were immediately picked up on a single that landed in front of the center fielder. Tied score! The medium-sized crowd in the stands gave the grinning hitter an ovation as he danced away from first.

A double play ended the threat, and the sagging infielders walked toward the dugout. "No sweat! No sweat!" Bucky clapped vigorously. "Get it back right now. Let's beat 'em!"

Demerest, glancing down at his lineup chart, chewed on his lip thoughtfully. The first-string shortstop was due up first, and he'd struck out badly the last two times. For whatever reason, he just didn't have his timing down yet. Making a mark on the sheet of paper, he looked in Bucky's direction. "Stone, go up there and pinch-hit."

"What?" Buddy, the wiry infielder, whirled around. "I'm not hitting?"

"Don't sweat it," the coach retorted, his tone of voice making it clear that he called the shots. "You did OK in the field, but we want to shake things up." He gave Bucky a little punch-gesture of encouragement. "Get on base for us."

Even though his and Dan's long hours of practice had

been for precisely this moment, Bucky still felt the butterflies as he put on a batting helmet. No wonder baseball
players described a late-inning pinch-hit assignment as the
toughest in the game. After six innings on the bench, you
simply weren't in the rhythm of the game. He felt a shiver
of nerves despite the warm April weather.

Stepping into the batter's box, he glanced out at the
mound. All game he'd been watching the opposing hurler's
moves, trying to pick up on any patterns. Almost always,
with the first batter of an inning, he wanted to get a strike—
but not a very good strike. About half the time his curve ball
had missed the zone, and he'd always come back with a
hard fastball to make sure he didn't fall behind 2-0.

"Miss that first one," he muttered to himself. "Then I'm
in the driver's seat."

"Go get him, Stone." Dan shouted out his encouragement. "Get on base and I'll knock you in."

The pitcher wound up and gave him the expected curve.
"Ball one!" The umpire hesitated for a moment before
announcing that the pitch had just missed the outside corner.
Bucky could feel his confidence rising. At batting practice
earlier that afternoon he'd been making good hard contact.

Taking a deep breath, he waved the bat back and forth.
"Come on," he breathed to himself. He wanted that fastball
bad. As the pitch came toward him, he felt that split second
of exhilaration. *Yeah!* Right in the zone he wanted, he
caught the pitch directly in his "wheelhouse." It was one of
those that a power hitter knew he'd crunched. The ball was
a distant arc as it sailed well over the left fielder's head and
bounced a solid 40 feet over the fence. It was a monster
homer, one that even Bucky knew was gone the moment he
made contact. Not one to stand at home plate and gloat, he
trotted evenly around the bases, trying to suppress the smile
threatening to break through. As he rounded third, he could

hear Dan screaming. "Yes! It's rolling into the ocean!"

The entire team was at the dugout entrance to give him high fives. "What a shot!" Even Buddy, the shortstop who'd been replaced, was grinning. "Good one, Stone. I'll admit I can't hit 'em that far myself."

The home run seemed to have paralyzed the home team. In the bottom of the final frame Chad got rid of the hitters with a total of four pitches. Bucky, watching from the dugout, gave a satisfied nod. As the players gathered around after the game, guys were still giving him little punches of approval. "Give the man the game ball," one of them said to Coach Demerest. "You ain't gonna get many homers bigger than that one."

Demerest watched in silence as Bucky and Dan went into the locker area and sank down in front of their lockers. "You and me, Stone," Dan repeated. "You and me."

A BLAST
FROM THE PAST

Just a trace of drizzle hung in the air as Bucky, Dan, and Julie did the last mile of their four-mile route. It was the first time Julie had joined them, but she was keeping up gamely with the two senior guys. "You doin' all right, hot thing?" Dan wanted to know.

"Sure." She wiped away some of the moisture beading on her forehead. "How much farther is it?"

" 'Bout a quarter mile is all." The last stretch near Dan's home was downhill all the way, and the trio sped up a bit, especially as the rain started coming down harder. They tumbled through the front door and into the living room just as it got really wet.

"Man, just in time." Dan went over to the refrigerator and pulled out a pitcher of ice-cold water. "Here, you guys."

Bucky glanced at his watch. "Man, we're not too fast today. I'm gonna be late for school."

"It's my fault." Julie wasn't even breathing hard, but she

held up her hand as if to admit a basketball foul. "Sorry."

"No, you did great." Bucky took a quick drink and then said goodbye to the couple. This afternoon was the Panthers' home opener, and he hadn't finished his physics assignment yet. The windows on the Toyota were badly fogged as he carefully drove over to Woodman Avenue.

Varsity baseball crowds at the high school usually weren't anything a sportswriter would notice, with Hampton Beach being more of a basketball town these days. But with the exciting win the last week to start them off right, the stands were nearly filled. A good number of local enthusiasts were sitting right down around home plate. A couple even had blank scoring reports out so they could chart every play.

"Don't these people have jobs?" Bucky laughed as he and Dan pegged hard liners back and forth to each other on the sidelines.

"Man, when I'm an old coot on Social Security, I'm going to go to a ballgame every day."

Both of the seniors were on the bench as the Panthers took the field for the top of the first inning. "Let's get 'em one, two, three!" Bucky told them as his teammates trotted out to their positions. "Dig in on defense!"

But again the pitching was less than memorable, as the visitors got a run in the first frame. Paul Crook, back in position in right field, misjudged a ball that was slicing away from him, and the team from Stockton took advantage of the two-base error.

"He's not very with it out there," Dan muttered as the run went up on the board. It took the Panthers until the third inning to catch up, and in the fourth the visitors promptly added two more.

"Now watch," Dan whispered to Bucky, scowling a bit. "Crook's not even paying attention. Right before the pitch, and he's just glazed over."

Moments later a lazy flyball sailed into right field. Paul did manage to make the routine catch, and immediately gave the ball a casual flip and began jogging toward the infield.

"Two outs!" Coach Demerest began shouting from the dugout. "There's only two outs! Wake up out there!" The runner on first, sizing up the situation, made a sprint for second base and slid in easily. "Come on!" The athletic director's face reddened. "Look alive!" He paced the dugout, muttering to everyone within earshot. "Unbelievable! We can't count to three!"

Bucky burrowed closer to Dan with a tight grin. "I'm scared," he murmured. "Save me."

"Dumb play." Dan was shaking his head. "Hope it doesn't cost us another run."

The inning ended harmlessly, and with one out in the bottom of the frame, the Panthers notched back-to-back singles. The crowd began to stir with the possible rally.

"Stone!" Coach Demerest motioned with his head toward the diamond. "Hit."

Bucky tried not to look startled. It was an unusual move, having one outfielder pinch-hit for another one during the middle innings. He didn't want to peek over at Paul, who had to be steaming.

"Go after 'em, Tiger." Dan gave him a slap of encouragement. "Ducks are out there on the pond, Stone," he advised, referring to the runners on base. "Go rescue them."

"It's RBI time!" Bucky recognized the voice of an older man, a diehard alumni fan who had even attended the road game the previous week. "Knock 'em in, Stone."

He hadn't noticed any predictable pattern with this pitcher, so simply dug in at the plate, determined to pick out his best pitch. Coach had always said, "I don't mind if you men even go after the first one. If you like it, pull the trigger. Be aggressive up there. Those pitchers can't get the idea that the first one is free for them."

And the first pitch was right where he liked them, thigh-high and on the inside half. With a vicious swing, he drove the pitch past the third-base bag and down the line. Fair ball! Both runs scored easily and Bucky went into second with a stand-up double.

"You're batting a thousand so far!" Dan gave him a big thumbs-up from his seat in the dugout. "My man!"

Moments later Bucky scooted hard for home on a short single to center. It was a risky play, but with a burst of extra speed he avoided the catcher's tag with a clever slide.

"Yeah!" Coach Demerest was the first one to greet him as he returned to the dugout bringing a Panther lead with him. "Heads-up baserunning!"

As the team made the third out, Dan tossed Bucky his glove. "Coach says you're in on defense too."

"Huh?" Bucky had thought it had been just a pinch-hitting assignment.

"Get in there." Dan gave him a little push. "Show 'em some leather."

Bucky jogged out to right field, still hearing some scattered applause from the fans on that side of the diamond as he found his spot. "Way to bring them back, Bucky," one of them called out.

The rest of the game went uneventfully as the Panthers held on to their lead. Two routine fly balls came his way, which he handled easily, and in the last inning Dan knocked in an insurance run with a long pinch-hit sacrifice fly up against the fence. The team felt a glow as they exchanged high fives.

"I'm not complaining," Dan told Bucky as they showered off. "We're getting plenty of playing time so far, and it's working out just fine." He flicked some soap at his friend. "'Specially you with three ribbies already. Demerest is going to want to adopt you and make you his heir or something."

Sure enough, the athletic director was waiting for them just outside the complex as they emerged. "Good job, men," he said pleasantly.

"Thanks, Coach." For a moment Dan looked past him, to see if Julie was waiting. "Two and zip already."

"I'd give anything to put you in the lineup all the time," he responded. "Are you sure you guys won't change your mind?"

Bucky hesitated. No, he and Dan weren't going to change their minds, but he didn't want to be flippant. "We sure like playing for you. But . . . we still can't play those two games. I'm awfully sorry." He glanced over at his friend. "I mean, we both are."

Coach Demerest nodded, frowning just a little bit. "OK," he said at last. With a short nod, he was gone.

"So we just keep on," Dan observed. "Fine with me." He scratched his head. "Wonder where my lady friend is. Guess she don't love me no more." He pointed over toward Bucky's Toyota. "Looks like things might be looking up for you, though."

Bucky glanced toward his little white compact and sucked in his breath. Lisa was standing there waiting for him.

What?

As he walked slowly toward her his mind raced. What did she want? What should he say? For a quick second his recent prayer flashed into his mind. As he looked at her now, her long hair blowing against her face, all his romantic determination came flooding back despite his best intentions.

He stopped a few feet away from her. "Hi."

"Hi." She looked down awkwardly at his bag. "Did you win?"

"Yeah. Beat them by two runs."

"That's good." She stood next to the door on the driver's side.

Bucky hesitated. "Do you, like, need a ride somewhere or anything?"

She gave a little shake of her head. "Huh uh. I was just . . . waiting for you."

He swallowed at the lump in his throat. "Well, you know I'm always in favor of that." *Lord, don't let me say anything too stupid! Please!*

"Do you have to be anywhere right now? Do you have to work?"

"Are you kidding?" A bit of confidence began to return. "Baseball players always have time for their loyal fans." He dug in his pocket for his keys. "Hang on, let me dump this stuff in the trunk." As he was putting things away, he peered over the top of the car at her. "Did you want to just . . . talk or something? Or get something to eat?"

"No, that's OK. Just . . . I want to talk."

Instinctively he took her arm and pointed toward the bleachers. The brief touch made him shiver. "OK then." He pointed. "The best Lisa-and-Bucky conversations always happened over there. Remember?"

"Yeah."

"'Course that was in the olden days."

The pair walked in silence over to the metal bleachers, now completely empty. In the distance Bucky could hear the *zip-zip-zip* of an automatic sprinkler as it crawled slowly away from them. He held out his hand and helped her up to the top level of the grandstand seats. "How's that?"

"Good." She sat and scooted a bit closer to him, an innocent, vulnerable move. For a long minute she gazed down at the sod below the bleachers, not speaking.

"Is everything OK?" he asked at last, his voice low.

Lisa nodded. "Yeah. I guess." She looked right at him.

"I'm glad you're in my government class."

It seemed like an odd remark. Ever since the transfer to Mr. Rojas' section, Lisa had stayed in the corner and he and Dan had parked on the second row. But he didn't pursue the thought with her.

"How's your mom?" he asked at last.

She shrugged, giving a little tug at her blouse as the wind momentarily blew it off her left shoulder. "She's all right. Kind of busy with work, so I don't see her very much."

They visited for a few minutes, talking about safe things. Bucky had never felt this way with Lisa before—safe again and yet tingling with a trace of the romantic impulses that undoubtedly nothing would ever erase in his heart. All he knew was that he didn't want the moment to end.

"I still think about you a lot," he said at last, hoping the admission wouldn't throw the conversation off course.

She gave him a smile. "I know, Bucky."

He gulped. "You do?"

"Sure." Lisa gave a little laugh that so reminded him of their freshman year it almost brought tears to his eyes. "I'm a woman." She put a bit of deliberate sultriness into her voice, and they both laughed a little.

"I felt so lousy after Hawaii," he finally confessed, breathing a silent prayer as he told her. "It was dumb to call you like that."

A school bell buzzed in the distance. Most of the campus was empty now as Bucky waited to see what she'd say. She looked right at him, her face tightening at the memory.

"I just . . . couldn't help it." He groped for the right words. "I had been thinking about you and just on an impulse went for it. But I caught you at a bad time, and I'm really sorry."

Again a long moment of quiet. Had he gotten into something he should have left alone? Bucky desperately wanted to know that God was directing whatever might happen next.

All at once Lisa slid over until she was right next to him. Wordlessly she reached out and clutched at his right arm until her cheek was against his shoulder. He flushed.

"I want to tell you what happened," she said at last. For a moment he thought he saw moisture in her eyes, but she was almost too close to see. He couldn't tell.

"OK."

Her fingers tightened, digging into his biceps. "It was something like January 2. Right?"

"Yeah."

She looked away from him for a minute, and when she turned her face back toward him, he noticed a tear trickling down her cheek.

"Oh, babe." It came out before he realized it. "Lisa, what . . . ?"

"I get a call from Steve . . . and then I get a call from you. Maybe 15 minutes apart."

So? He waited, but it didn't seem like she was going to say any more. Reaching with his left hand, he moved his fingers against hers. "What happened?"

She didn't shift away, but something inside of her stiffened. "Sorry," he whispered, waiting.

At last she took a deep breath, her voice catching as she spoke. "Well, it's kind of hard," she said. "You tell some guy, 'I think I'm pregnant!' . . . and he says to you back, 'So? How could you be so stupid, you dumb . . .'" The epithet hung on her lips, but she didn't say the word.

Bucky's mind reeled. *What did you say?* A violent knot began to form in his stomach.

"And then he hangs up." She looked at him, her eyes flooding with tears. "I'm crying, and he tells me I'm a stupid . . . you know. And then he hangs up." All at once, her slim body was shaking as she buried her face in her knees. "After everything we'd . . . done together . . . he just hung up on me."

Her raw pain tore at him. Despite how shocked he was, Bucky found tears in his eyes too. He looked through them at the top of her head as her muffled sobs continued. "It's OK," he whispered, repeating the words over and over. He really didn't know what else to say.

For at least a minute there was nothing but the muffled sobs. He racked his brain, trying to take in what he'd just heard. *Lisa and Steve.* Something inside of him involuntarily railed at the thought. How could she! Then he remembered how he'd almost failed with Deirdre, and suddenly he felt flooded with shame. Carefully pulling his right arm free, he slid it around Lisa and held her close. For just a moment, the sobs intensified as she buried her face in his shoulder. "Oh, Bucky . . ."

After a long painful silence, she finally pulled away a little bit. "I must look a mess." Her voice was shaky.

"It's OK." He reached in his pocket but realized he didn't have a handkerchief. "Sorry," he murmured.

Lisa took a deep, trembling breath. "I didn't really mean to tell you all of that. But . . . I guess, deep down, I did. Or I had to. Or something."

His voice was carefully gentle when he responded. "So what happened?"

Lisa looked away from him, toward the distant hills on the other side of I-80. "Well, after all of that, it turned out to be a false alarm. I mean, yeah, I'd been late. Really late. And then when I took that, you know, drugstore test you can buy, it said I was too. So that's when I went crazy, of course. But about a week later . . . obviously, I wasn't."

Bucky waited, trying to understand it all.

"But by then everything had collapsed."

"With Steve?"

"Yeah. *Steve.*" She said the name with a grimace, almost choking up again.

"Did he ever call back?"

"Nope." She wiped at her nose. "Not a single time. Not to find out what happened, not to say, 'I love you,' 'I'm sorry,' 'Lisa, can I help you get through this?' nothing."

"Man." He turned to face her. "I'm so sorry."

"Well, that wasn't all," she continued. "Right when I thought I was, you know, pregnant, I was stupid enough to tell one of the kids here. You know that real loud girl in government, the one on the front row who keeps shooting off her mouth?"

"Yeah." He swallowed hard.

"Her. Like, how stupid could I have been? But she caught me in a vulnerable moment, and I told her. Next thing I know, half the school was in on it." Her lip trembled for a moment and she clenched her fist. "You wouldn't believe some of the stuff I heard. From girls in the locker room after gym. From *guys.* I heard some real sweet stuff from guys."

Bucky didn't know what to say. "I'm just glad you're OK now."

"A couple of them brought you into it," she told him, shaking her head. "Like, 'Who's the helpful dude, honey?' And then wondering if it was you."

"Me?"

"I don't know why. Somebody remembered . . . us . . . from before, I guess."

Bucky digested that thought, his brow furrowing.

At last Lisa pulled herself free and stood up, adjusting her blouse and pulling her hair away from her face. "Anyway, that's it," she told him. "That's how things are going for your little, almost got baptized once, ex-girlfriend

Lisa Nichols." She paused. "Aren't you proud of me?"

He didn't say anything.

The slim girl's voice tightened as she thrust her fists into the pockets of her tight jeans. "Wouldn't you like me back now? All of a sudden, I'm real available."

Slowly he stood and faced her, balancing on the narrow metal beam. For a moment he didn't say anything, but then he reached out and took her hand in his. "I don't care about that," he murmured, his voice low, not meaning a word of what he was saying.

CHAPTER 8

BEAT BY YOUR OWN BROTHER

Although he had a big English assignment due the next morning, Bucky simply pushed it to one side. He'd take a 10 percent hit in his grade for it being late, but he had to think. After supper he quickly did the dishes and then excused himself.

"I'm going for a walk, Mom."

Jenny Stone looked at him curiously. "Everything OK?"

The look in his eyes must have told her something, because she didn't press him.

It was a beautiful April evening in the Bay Area, with the soft twilight of daylight savings just kicking in. But Bucky's mind was in turmoil as he did the extended three-mile loop that the Stone family sometimes toured on Sabbath evenings. He replayed the afternoon's conversation.

Lisa, the girl who'd always mattered more than anybody else . . . had slept with another guy. The battle he'd almost lost himself—she *had* lost.

"But how can you blame her?" he muttered to himself, hating his thoughts. After all, he was a born-again Christian, the most dedicated believer at Hampton Beach High School, and he'd just about given in himself. What right did he have to expect someone like Lisa to make it? The fact that she'd kind of lost her way spiritually wasn't even really her fault—it was the move to Seattle.

And then there was the sudden, jarring return of all of his emotional feelings. In at least one sense, the Lisa he had known before had returned. She had come to him! The girl had wanted to talk, to share, to sit close to him. He still remembered the softness of her cheek pressed against his shoulder, her hand clutching at his arm. Did he still love her? Could he possibly think about putting the horrible experience behind him and starting all over?

Angrily he kicked at a pebble on the sidewalk, and it skipped away from him, bouncing crazily until it hit a sprinkler head on someone's lawn. It was impossible not to have a mental picture of Lisa with Steve. And the sensation caused his fists to tighten, until he remembered again how the path to physical intimacy had seemed so easy for him as well. Stuff like this happened. It was wrong, but it was easy too . . . and it happened.

As he slowly looped back toward Woodman Avenue, a strange kind of anger began to fill him. He didn't really feel it toward Lisa—at least, he didn't think so. She was so vulnerable, still so . . . *good*. Maybe he could never really hate her or even be mad. But his face tightened as a quiet rage against *sin* seemed to settle in his mind.

How could Satan use love the way he did, and twist it around until people were in tears like Lisa had been? To feel so used afterwards, so carelessly discarded? Again he wondered what might have happened if God hadn't intervened to protect him in Room 1929 in Honolulu a few short months before? What might have happened to his own spiritual relationship with God? How would he have felt going down the elevator to the hotel lobby, knowing he'd betrayed Jesus? The little glow of sexual release stacked up against all Jesus had done for him these last four years. Bucky weighed the two and felt sick. Tears moistened his cheeks and he brushed angrily at them.

"Help me," he groaned, half-aloud. "Help me to be a *man*." Somehow he knew that God still needed him. He glanced up at the moonlit night, trying to feel that He was still up there. "A spiritual man," he added. The whispered prayer didn't sound stupid, but like the biggest challenge he'd ever considered.

After the next practice Coach Demerest called Dan and Bucky into his cramped office. Baseball magazines and grade sheets were all over his desk, and he brushed them to the side as he motioned them to sit.

"Look," he said without fanfare, "I can't keep things going like this." He cleared his throat and glanced from one to the other. "I've decided to go ahead and play the two of you on a regular basis for whatever games you can attend."

Bucky gulped. Wow! It was a complete reversal from what Demerest had said before. "That's great! I mean, sure, Coach."

"Yeah," Dan put in. "Thanks!"

Something inside Bucky wanted to ask why the athletic director had changed his mind, but he decided that wasn't really his business.

"I guess I may as well tell you why," Demerest said, as if reading their thoughts. "You guys know what I said about needing the same starting lineup, and only using starters who can give me, you know, themselves for the whole schedule."

Dan nodded. "Uh huh."

"I still feel that way," the coach told them. "Except that my other obligation is to put the best athletes I can on the field in every game."

Bucky felt a bit of glow at the compliment. The older man looked right at him as he continued. "And the two of you are in better shape, play better, know the game better, and—well, just about everything—than anyone else on the varsity squad. And everybody knows it."

The two absorbed what the coach had said. "What about those two games?" Dan managed.

"I guess we'll do without." Demerest gave a little shake of his head. "I talked on the phone with Brayshaw the other day, and he told me, 'Don't even try to change Litton and Stone's minds. They'll never do it.' So I guess that's that."

Bucky shifted uneasily in his seat. "I . . . guess we just don't want to have the team resent us."

"I don't think they do," the athletic director said quickly. "Like I said, they all know the two of you are our best players. So they know fair is fair. Plus they want to win." He managed a little smile. "Sure, they'd all like to be starters, but any ballplayer worth a nickel is glad when a teammate comes in and hits a monster homer in the seventh to win the game."

"What about playoffs?" Dan again.

"I don't know the schedule yet. Probably two more weeks before it even gets determined by the district office. I know it's an abbreviated format now, and latest word is, it may not even involve Friday night. So let's wait and see on that."

The Panthers' third game, another road contest at San Ramon, gave the two Christian athletes their first opportunity as varsity starters. Bucky had always known that he wouldn't bat a thousand all season, but he did manage to go two for four at the plate, including a timely single up the middle in the last inning to help ice the contest. And both he and Dan played flawless baseball in right and center field. Dan, in particular, brought groans to the frustrated home crowd as he threw a runner out at the plate with a one-hop screamer.

"Good job!" Bucky grinned in satisfaction as they took the three-run victory into the locker room. He walked over to where Paul was just unbuttoning his jersey. "Hey, Crook. Good hit there at the end." The outfielder, now relegated to the bench because of Bucky's promotion, had also gotten a pinch-hit single in the last inning when he'd batted for the pitcher.

The other player glanced up, still a trace of resentment on his face. "Thanks," he muttered.

Bucky edged a little closer. "Listen, man," he managed, "I'm sorry about this stuff. I mean, sure, I like playing. Just like you. But I know how it feels." He knew it was an awkward overture, but didn't know what else to do.

The other senior hesitated, then gave a little shrug. "It's OK. I mean, you deserve the spot."

"Well, look. Let's just be a team, man. Every chance you get to play and hit and . . . whatever, I'm all for it."

"Thanks." Paul's gaze followed Bucky as he returned to his own locker.

As they walked together out to the team bus, Dan suddenly turned toward Bucky. "You see who our next game is against?"

"Huh uh."

"Davis. And your friend Jeff Hilliard."

"Are you sure?"

"Yup. I wonder if he'll be pitching?"

"He gave me his phone number," Bucky said, remembering. "I guess I could call him."

"Are you kidding? And ask him if he's pitching?"

"Sure, why not?"

"I don't know. Just seems weird. 'We're coming up to cream you, and just hope you're the pitcher of record when we do.'"

Bucky thought about that. "Actually, I don't know if I want to face him or not face him." He shrugged. "Guess it doesn't matter."

As the Panthers suited up for their second consecutive road game, he glanced out at the stands. With Davis being quite a ways up the interstate, the stands held only a handful of Hampton Beach fans. And sure enough, over on the home-field side of the diamond, he could see Jeff warming up as the starting pitcher. A strange feeling came over him, as the scene from two years ago flashed into his mind once again. It was strange how the resentment from that hot afternoon back home had vanished.

Just before the game he and Dan walked over to where Jeff had just finished his pitching routine. "How you doin'?" Dan said.

"OK, I guess." Hilliard grinned. "Here we go." He paused. "Good luck to you guys. I mean that."

"Sure. You too." Bucky was still tugging at his batting gloves. "Looked like some heat you were throwing. Go easy on us, OK?"

Jeff glanced around. "You guys want to have a prayer or something?"

Something inside Bucky did a flip-flop. This couldn't be happening. "Yeah." He and Dan bowed their heads as the opposing pitcher from Davis said a short prayer. "And Father, bless these two friends of mine," Jeff said, his eyes tightly closed. "Protect us all during this game. Help us to honor Your holy name by our attitudes and how we play. And . . . Lord Jesus, I just want to thank You again that You

gave me this chance to ask forgiveness and gain Bucky and
Dan as my brothers in Christ."

Bucky was flushed with emotion as the two Hampton
Beach players returned to their dugout. "Unbelievable,"
Dan muttered. "Absolutely unbelievable."

"How are we gonna go up there and hit off him now?"

Suddenly Dan laughed. "Oh, no problem there. I'm still
gonna nail that boy's pitches."

But it was Jeff who had the last laugh, as he hurled a
complete-game shutout, beating the Panthers two to nothing on only three hits. Bucky managed a harmless bases-
empty single in the sixth inning, but Dan struck out twice
and didn't get the ball out of the infield.

"Man!" The stocky player was grumpy as he stalked
into the locker room. "I couldn't hit the side of a barn
today!" He tossed his glove onto the floor and gave it a little kick. "That Hilliard is wicked, Stone."

"I know it." Bucky had visions of getting shut down in
a crucial playoff game against the big Christian hurler. "At
least today, he was just plain better than us."

Coach Demerest came over and put a hand on Litton's
shoulder. "Don't worry about it," he advised. "That Hilliard
was in a zone, that's all. There wasn't nobody going to hit
him today, not with that sinker he had. One of the guys here
told me he isn't usually that good."

"What's their record?"

"Three and one, just like us."

Outside the locker room a reporter from the school
newspaper was waiting. "Are you Stone?"

"Yeah."

She tugged at a strand of hair. "Everyone says our
team and you guys are the best. What'd you think of the
game today?"

"Well, you saw it. Hilliard shut us down."

"Think you can beat him next time?"

"I hope so."

The student paused. "Some kids were saying something about him and you and that other guy all praying together. Before the game. Did that really happen?"

He nodded slowly.

"So . . . how? I mean, just out of the blue?"

Choosing his words carefully, Bucky described in very brief detail what had happened two years ago, and how reconciliation between the two Christians had finally taken place. The young girl listened carefully, scribbling down a few notes.

"But you ought to ask Jeff," he finally told her. "He goes to school here. It'd be a better story from him. I mean, he's your guy."

"I guess you're right." She shut her notebook. "But I never heard anything like that before."

"I better run," Bucky said suddenly. "I think our bus is about ready to leave."

It was a thoughtful ride back home as Bucky reflected on the pregame prayer and then the intensely competitive game itself. Jeff was a completely professional pitcher, hard-driving and totally absorbed during the game. And yet . . . a beautiful, compassionate Christian. A prayer—and then a three-hitter. As the miles slipped by, he commented about it to Dan. "Man, that's what I want for us too," he confessed.

"Yeah." Still stinging a bit about "drawing the collar" with no hits that afternoon, Dan nodded. "He was good all right."

It was late that evening when the phone rang. Dad picked it up in the garage and then opened the door a bit. "Bucky? For you."

For a moment he thought about Lisa and the unresolved problems she had. "Hello?"

"Stone?" The voice sounded familiar. "It's Jeff. You know, from the game."

"Oh yeah." He grinned to himself. "Called to rub it in, huh? You kicked our tails pretty good, man."

"I know. Sorry about that—I just got lucky."

"Yeah, *right.*"

"Listen, I know it's kind of late. But I just got a whole row of tickets to Sunday's game. You know the Giants have that big double-header."

"Against Colorado?"

"Yeah. And you know how those guys can hit. Do you and Litton want to go?"

He hesitated for only a moment. "As far as I know, sure. Our next game's not until Tuesday, so Monday's light."

"Great! I'm coming right through there, so I could pick you guys up and everything."

Bucky hung up the receiver with a grin. "This is one *weird* school year."

CHAPTER 9

BLEACHERS AND NEW BEGINNINGS

It was an overcast afternoon at 3COM Park as the four young men watched the endless baseball action. The orange-hued ballpark was probably three-quarters filled as San Francisco fans took advantage of the rare chance to see two games for the price of one. The Giants took the first game by an easy 9-1 score, and grabbed two quick runs in the first inning of the second contest.

"Why can't they play like this all the time?" Dan had his feet propped up on the seat in front of him. The corporate tickets Jeff had come up with were great, close to the field on the third-base side.

"Yo! Hot dog!" Jeff motioned to a vendor. "You guys want one?"

Bucky shook his head. Already he and Jeff had discussed a couple of Adventist ideas, but this probably wasn't the time to launch into a sermon on the benefits of vegetarianism.

The second game settled into a slow pitchers' duel, and Jeff plied his new friends with questions. "Stone, I hear what you're saying," he said at last, "but I don't see how it can be right. On that Saturday thing, anyway. That's the first thing they taught me in my beginner's Bible class at Calvary—that we're saved by grace. I mean, like, totally. Jesus does it all, and our works are nothing."

"I'm not disagreeing," Bucky interjected. "We think that too."

"So why do you *have* to worship on Saturday then? If it doesn't save you, then what does it do?"

The young Adventist shifted in his seat, grinning at Jeff. "You better watch it, Hilliard," Dan put in. "He'll whup you on this stuff."

"I ain't afraid."

"Well, here's how I look at it," Bucky said. "Jesus died on the cross, and so I'm saved. Right?"

"Amen, man." Jeff was suddenly serious.

"And He says about a million times, 'If you love Me, keep My commandments.' 'You're My friends if you do what I command.' And then Paul saying stuff like, 'Shall we dump the law? No way! We uphold the law.' I mean, that's all through the New Testament."

"Yeah, but that's the law of love. Love God and love your neighbor." Jeff pointed at Bucky, then suddenly jerked his head back toward the playing field as a Giant home run sailed over the fence. "The Sabbath and stuff like that ended at Calvary."

"I don't think that's right. Jesus told His own disciples, 'When you flee from Jerusalem'—and that happened in 70 A.D. or somewhere around then—'pray that you won't have to go on the Sabbath day.' And Paul worshiped on Sabbath a long time after Jesus was resurrected and went back to heaven and everything."

The other student thought about that. "Well, OK, but how about this? Maybe it's just OK for everyone to keep whatever day they want to choose. I know at Calvary Church, when they talk about Adventists, they just say, 'Well, great. They want to worship on Saturday; fine. We worship on Sunday, and they worship on Saturday, and they're our brothers in Christ.'"

"I feel that way too," Bucky shrugged. "To a point, anyway. But I can tell you this. I don't think in Eden that God ever intended to say to Adam and Eve, 'Well, hey, pick some day to worship Me. Whatever you decide. If you want to worship on Saturday, and maybe your kids on Sunday, and some of your other neighbors on Tuesday . . . whatever you want.'" He shook his head, rejecting the idea. "The whole point was to worship together. All as one community, one body in Jesus. I still think that's what God wants. And He said the seventh day."

The teams traded places as the third out was recorded. Sam, who'd been listening intently, suddenly leaned forward. "I can tell you what it means to me."

"Go for it." Jeff turned the other direction and faced the PUC freshman.

"Well, it's like this to me. I just want to follow Jesus *totally*. Not holding back anything, or looking for a loophole. He says, 'Obey Me,' and I want to make that a thousand-percent deal."

"Absolutely." Jeff nodded his assent.

"And for me that involves everything. All 10 commandments, because Jesus asks us to. All 10, because He kept all 10. And especially when you read in Revelation, man, and how the people of God in the last days, they keep the commandments with, like, *fierce* loyalty. For them it's like a mission." He swallowed hard, thinking about it. "That's what I want."

The student from Davis looked from one to the other. "Man, that's heavy stuff," he managed. "You guys really mean it, don't you?"

"For sure." Dan tugged at Bucky's jersey. "Come on, Stone. Time for the seventh-inning stretch. 'Take me out to the ballgame.' You know I can sing prettier than you."

It was a sunburned but happy ride back to Hampton Beach. Sam didn't have to get back to PUC until Monday evening, and the four guys stopped off at Taco Bell for a late supper to celebrate the Giants' sweep. They'd pretty much talked themselves out of theological questions, Bucky agreed, and they chatted about more trivial things as they devoured the big pile of seven-layer burritos.

"Good luck with your games, man," Dan told Jeff, shaking hands with the tall senior just before he pulled back onto the road. "Long as you're not playing us, Stone and I are pulling for your team all the way."

"We may get each other in the playoffs then."

The chunky centerfielder waved a fist in Jeff's face. "Revenge!"

Bucky spotted a note taped to the refrigerator as he slipped into the darkened house on Woodman Avenue. He frowned as he flipped on the kitchen light and glanced at his watch. It was unusual for his parents to already be in bed this early. "Lisa called," the note said. "9:15. Call back if not too late. Mom." She'd written a phone number at the bottom of the sheet.

It was 10:00 now, he noted, peeking at his watch a second time. Should he go ahead and call? He slipped over to the wall phone, trying to be quiet. A moment later Lisa was on the line.

"I hope it's not too late to call," he told her.

"Huh uh. It's OK."

He hesitated. "Are you OK? What's up?"

Several seconds went by before she answered, and when she did, it came out sounding tremulous. "I just . . . can I come see you? Or something?"

"Are you OK?" he repeated gently.

A pause. "No. Not really. I'm just . . . all mixed up about everything."

"My folks have gone to bed already," Bucky said, lowering his voice. "But I can come over there."

"Huh uh. I don't think . . . you know, my mom and stuff."

"Well, what then?"

"I don't know."

He thought hard. "We could meet at the school. Where we were the other day. I don't think they ever lock it up before midnight."

"Do you mind?" she said at last, her voice still shaking. "Please?"

"Give me 10 minutes, babe." It was strange how the little word of endearment came out so naturally despite the mixed-up emotions he still had for her.

"OK," she whispered.

He hung up the phone, feeling quivery inside. What was it now? What was going to happen? Breathing a prayer to God, he scribbled a second note on the back of the first one. He put it where Mom would find it just in case she came downstairs and found him still gone.

The amber lights around the high school were glowing their disapproval as his Toyota crept into the parking lot next to the athletic field. Only one other car occupied it, and Lisa was waiting inside with the doors locked. She eased the door open and stepped out just as he walked over. Without speaking, she slipped into his embrace, burying her face in his chest.

"It's OK," he whispered. "Whatever the matter is, God'll help you. And me too."

A minute or two went by before she pulled herself free. "Can we just go back over there or somewhere?"

"Sure." With his arm still around her, Bucky led her over to the same grandstands, now immersed in inky darkness. A distant set of lights illuminated the parking lot with the two lonely cars at the far end.

"How are you feeling about . . . you know, everything that happened to you?" He asked the question gently.

"Bad." She turned away from him for a moment. "Sometimes I feel even worse now than I did back then."

"How come?"

"I don't know." Her eyes moistened. "I mean, I don't . . . *want* Steve anymore. After what happened. But I feel so lonely. And *wrong*." She turned to face him. "I screwed up so bad!"

Bucky waited before answering. "Yeah. I guess. But God's already forgiven you."

"Has He?" The words came out angrily. "You say that like, 'Well, no problem! God is love. Blah blah blah.' But I swear none of that stuff is true for me."

He reached over and pulled her closer. "You know *me*," he told her. "And I'm telling you, God is there. He loves you as much as He ever did. That stuff with . . . Steve . . . He still loves you. Sure, it was wrong. But it's done. It's over, and He forgives you. It's like it didn't happen."

She looked at him, her eyes wet. "But it did happen. You can say all that because it didn't happen to you."

A painful thought jabbed its way to the surface of his mind. "But it did happen to me," he said at last after a moment of stark silence.

"What?"

"It did happen," he winced. Carefully, remembering

with every word, he told her about Hawaii and his experience with Deirdre.

"Well, there you go," she put in. "You almost did, but you didn't."

Bucky hung his head in shame. "But I was right there. In my mind, it had already happened. I mean, no, not the whole physical thing. But I was ready and willing—and I'm a Christian. I should have been a million miles away from a temptation like that, and I wasn't. But God forgave me too." His eyes searched hers, desperate to see any sign that she was hearing what he was saying. "He loves you so much."

Lisa stared dully down at her shoes, her shoulders sagging with the weight. "I'd give anything to have what you . . ."

A sudden noise in the parking lot caused them both to turn to see what it was. They spotted a city patrol car wheeling up next to Bucky's car, its spotlight flickering across the field. Then a man in uniform got out and slowly began walking toward the bleachers.

"Hope we're not in trouble," Bucky whispered.

The heavy footsteps crunched as the officer approached. Bucky moved down several levels so the man could see him better. "What's going on here?" the policeman said.

"We're just . . . talking. We both go to school here."

"It's after hours," he snapped with authority and beamed a flashlight in Lisa's direction, taking in the situation. Suddenly the beam fell on Bucky's face. "Wait a minute. Aren't you . . . Stone? Bucky Stone?"

"Yeah." He blushed.

"OK. I helped write up that report on that kid, the ballplayer who was busted for shaving points. A year ago. You helped us with that, didn't you?"

"Uh huh."

The officer reflected for a moment, then switched off

the powerful beam. "It's OK, Stone. Take your time. But be out of here by midnight, OK?"

"Sure. Thanks."

The red taillights disappeared down the access road as he returned to sit next to Lisa. "Where were we?"

"Oh, just crying on each other's shoulders." She gave him a wan smile. "You're so sweet to do this." All at once tears filled her eyes again. "I never deserved a guy like you."

"Don't say that," he told her. "I always felt so lucky to have you."

A nearby church chimed 11:00, the bells echoing dolefully in the night air. "So what do I do?" Lisa asked.

"About what?"

"How do I get past all this? It just always pounds at me. 'You messed up. You gave away your . . . virginity. It's gone forever, and you can't get it back.' Nobody cares. Nobody gives a rip about me anymore." She slammed her fists down on her knees in anger. "Everything's so unfair."

His heart in his throat, he reached over and held both of her fists. "Come on," he said. "Look at me."

Lisa turned to face him, her face wet. "OK, I'm looking. Tell me something to fix it all."

"I can't dig up some other message," he told her. "All I got is the one." Now his own eyes were brimming as he breathed a prayer. "Babe, God loves you. He does. I swear He does." He reached out and traced a hand along her face. "And *I* love you."

Time seemed to freeze itself in place as the four words hung in the air between them. "Don't say that," she whispered. "Bucky, please. Don't say it if you don't mean it."

He hesitated. *Did* he mean it? He'd asked God to help him reach out to Lisa, to care about her in the right way—in heaven's way. Did he love her now? *Something* was certainly welling up in his heart at this very moment. This girl next to him—with the tears in her eyes, the lost look on her face—he felt something, but was it love or a kind of missionary impulse? Or did it matter anymore?

"I love you," he said again, feeling the validity of the words grow in his heart as he repeated them. Very slowly he pulled her closer and kissed her.

It was a short, tender kiss, kind of a mixed-up gesture, and they both knew it. He pulled back, feeling the wetness from her cheeks. All the memories from the past three years seemed to be in his mind at once: Lisa moving away, the tumultuous relationship with Deirdre, the aborted trip to Seattle, a fizzy-personality redhead named Tracy, plus all the ups and downs of holding onto a Christian faith in an MTV world.

And now Lisa was here again. Was everything he'd hoped for coming true after all? Could he carve out a brand-new relationship with her? One that had Jesus at its center?

"Bucky . . ." Her eyes were searching his, trying to figure out what was happening.

For a moment he held back, a pause that almost made him ache. And then all at once the reserve broke. He clutched her fiercely, kissing her again and again. Now she returned his kisses, pulling him closer and even closer.

"I love you too," she repeated, burying her face in his jacket. "I love you."

CHAPTER 10

JUST LIKE THAT
ETHIOPIAN GUY

The next few days at high school were a kind of strange but not unpleasant dream. Lisa now sat next to Bucky and Dan in Mr. Rojas' government class, and a couple times at lunch, Julie joined them to make it a foursome. But despite the intensity of Sunday evening, Bucky could tell things still weren't like before.

He and Dan talked about it right before the Tuesday afternoon Panther home game. "Well, look, Stone, you know she's still fragile about . . . God and stuff. That's what it is."

"Yeah, maybe."

"I mean, until she decides to become a Christian—born again, the whole works—you're kind of like three-fourths of a couple."

It was a dumb analogy, and Bucky couldn't help but grin despite his frustration. "I didn't think you knew that much about fractions."

"Shut up. I got a B$^+$ in that stuff."

The taller athlete finished lacing up his cleats and stood to his full height. "Well, let me ask you this then, smart guy. Should I be going with her? You know how I made myself that rule about never dating someone who wasn't a Christian." Bucky shrugged. "'Course, I've broken that rule about five times already, and look where it's gotten me."

Dan shook his head vigorously. "This is different, Stone. You know Lisa's going to make the right decision. And she needs you to help get her to the finish line." He picked up his glove. "In the meantime, you and I have a few home runs to hit."

Bucky did indeed crunch a big three-run homer in the fifth inning to seal the Panther's fourth win. "That's more like it," he grunted to Dan as they trotted off the field. "I guess we're marvelous athletes except when we're facing Hilliard on the mound."

"Yeah, I don't know what we're going to do about that. Maybe he'll go to the mission field in the next month. I could always suggest it to him. I don't see how he could beat us from Nigeria."

"Good show, guys." Coach Demerest clapped each of the athletes on the back as they gathered around for the postgame diagnosis. "No errors, and we left only two on base. That's clutch hitting." He glanced over at Bucky. "And you know what they say: good pitching plus three-run homers usually spells a W."

A murmur of assent went through the locker room as one of the ballplayers right behind Bucky gave him a generous thump of congratulations. "'Course, we're on again this Friday for one of our two night games," the athletic director continued. "So two of our big guns will be missing." He made the observation without any apparent resentment. "You men know that Litton and Stone won't be on the squad, so we have to just pump it up and compensate." He glanced at his clipboard. "The rest of you bring some extra lumber. Crook, you and Randy are back in, and I hear Concord's been hitting the ball right up against the fences, so be ready for a lot of action. But we're a good hitting team too, and I sure want to come out of that contest with a 5-1 record." He clapped his hands together twice. "OK, guys, that's it."

Just before taking his shower, Bucky went over to where Paul Crook was stripping off his jersey. "Listen, Crook."

"Yeah, what?" The response came out muffled as he pulled the fabric over his head.

"Well, just . . . good luck Friday. I hope you hit some smokers."

The other player weighed the words, wondering if Bucky meant them. Then he gave a casual shrug. "Thanks, I guess. You guys are off to church, huh?"

Bucky grinned. "Something like that."

Paul stood up and measured the other ballplayer. "Fine with me. The more prayer meetings you go to, the more I get to play."

It was an awkward moment, and Bucky didn't know what to say. Paul, sensing the same, gave a dismissive wave of his hand. "Don't mind me, Stone. Yeah, sure, I'll do my best."

"Go for it."

Lisa was waiting outside the athletic complex, and they chatted for the few spare minutes Bucky had before driving over to the bank. Dan and Julie gave them a wave as his sporty blue Camaro thundered out of the parking lot. Bucky smiled to himself. Despite the tentative nature of the new relationship, it still felt awfully good.

"What are you smirking about?"

He gave her an innocent look. "Seems to me, back in the good old days, victorious ballplayers always got kissed

by the most beautiful women at Hampton Beach High
School. Don't tell me that tradition's gone glub-glub-glub
down the drain."

Lisa laughed. "Oh, come here." She gave him a very
chaste little peck on the cheek.

"Maybe you're forgetting I hit a three-run homer,"
he reminded.

"Oh." Another kiss, this one more generous.

"That's more like it." A warm glow filled the Toyota as
he drove over to First California Bank for the abbreviated 90-
minute shift. The savings institution closed a half hour after
he arrived, but there was always the posting of deposits to
be done and various other clerical duties. He kept thinking
about the Friday night contest—a big game against the varsity squad from Concord. All the teams were good this year,
but Concord and Davis seemed to have the toughest line-
ups. Jeff Hilliard's team shared first place with the Panthers
at 4-1, and even this early in the season, any loss hurt a lot.

Friday evening after supper, the entire Stone family
went for a short walk to the park. He'd promised to go over
and see Lisa, but that wasn't until about 8:00. Rachel Marie
and he did a few lazy circles on the tiny merry-go-round
and watched as the sun slowly set behind the hills. It was
a spectacular sunset, with just a few clouds on the horizon.

Bucky tried to picture in his mind the electric *zap!* as
huge floodlights went on at the Concord ballpark. Because
Friday games were the only night contests, he'd never
played under the lights except for those few disastrous moments his freshman year. But he'd been to plenty of night
games at "the *former* Candlestick Park," as San Francisco
purists disdainfully called 3COM. And he knew the jolt of
excitement as the home team took the field and nervous
visiting players got ready to step up to the plate in front of
a huge crowd of hostile student fans.

"Do you wish you were playing baseball?" Rachel Marie asked as they climbed off the merry-go-round.

Her older brother looked startled. "Oh, well, I guess I wish it wasn't tonight. 'Course I like to play. But not on Sabbath."

"They'll never win without you playing, Bucky," she assured him. "Don't worry."

"I *want* them to win," he protested, wondering deep down if he was telling the truth.

It was a little after 8:00 before he kissed his little sister and climbed into the Toyota for the short drive to Lisa's. "Have a good time, honey." Mom waved as he pulled out onto Woodman Avenue.

He felt a tingle of nervous anticipation as he pulled up in front of the Nichols' home a few minutes later. Lisa's mom had never liked him, and hadn't bothered to be diplomatic about the fact. But she greeted him at the door and invited him in.

"She'll be down in a minute," she told him, brushing away a strand of hair. The older woman had a kind of tired resignation in her face that seemed to say, "I'd be on your case, young man, but it's just not worth the bother anymore." She went back into the kitchen without further conversation.

A few moments later Lisa came out of the darkened hallway and into the living room. "Hi."

Bucky grinned. "Hi."

"Want to go out for a little while?"

He nodded. "Sure."

She turned her head and called out, "Mom, we're going down to the park."

The woman didn't answer, and Lisa gave a noncommittal shrug. "Let's go."

As they walked in wordless silence toward the small city park she took his hand. Traffic was light in the residential area, and they did a slow, comfortable circle around the outer perimeter of the greenbelt.

"It's sure great having you back here," he told her.

"Yeah." She gave his hand a little squeeze. "I guess."

"No guessing about it. I'm really glad."

Sitting on one of the concrete-slab benches, they watched as a couple of stray dogs snapped at each other in the distant moonlight. "Dogs are so dumb sometimes," he murmured.

They chatted about school for a few minutes before she suddenly shifted around and faced him. "I've got to ask you something."

"Yeah, what?"

She took a deep breath. "This is going to sound dumb. But here goes." A moment of hesitation. "What do I have to do to . . . be a Christian again? Like you."

Bucky's heart began to pound in his chest. *What?* He'd figured it might take months for Lisa to begin to realize what she needed. And here, on their very first Sabbath together, she was already asking.

"Are you serious?"

She nodded, her dark eyes intently boring into his. "Uh huh."

He reflected on the question. *The* question. It was strange that a hundred answers flooded his thinking. "Do you believe in God?"

"Yeah." A frown. "I guess."

"No, do you *really* believe in Him?"

"What do you mean?"

He glanced away from her, remembering. "When I was 8, my mom had Rachel Marie. And they were just starting to let dads and even other brothers and sisters go into the delivery room."

"And you watched it?"

"Uh huh." He felt in awe as he recalled the event. "I saw my own sister . . . come out. I mean, her little face. And I was just, you know, a dumb kid. Eight years old. But I saw that baby *face*—and I knew even then, stuff like that didn't just happen. It wasn't just dumb luck that makes a human being start growing. And then when I became a Christian, it really hit me hard: man, that's God."

"Yeah." Lisa nodded. "I never thought of that."

He went on. "Anyway, for me it's all a train of logic. I believe in God. And I believe He's good, that He tells the truth. So when He says Jesus is His own Son, I believe that too. And then I believe everything Jesus teaches. *Everything.* God is true; Jesus is true; His teachings are true. I can't just jump off that train halfway down the track. And that's why I'm not just a Christian, but a Seventh-day Adventist." He paused again, searching her face. "I have to follow it all the way. It's really as simple as that."

She slid her hand up his arm until it was resting in the crook of his elbow. He could feel her fingers tighten as she thought about what he'd said. "Bucky, are you sure? Are you sure it's right? I don't mean the Adventist stuff, but just . . . being a Christian." She swallowed hard. "I've got to be sure."

The question made him quiver. "Babe . . . don't decide because I say so." He shook his head. "Because I've been a rotten Christian a lot of times."

"I don't think so."

"Well, I have been. Anyway, being a Christian is *your* decision. You've got to think about it, and you've got to be the one who weighs all the evidence and then either give your life to it . . . or don't." The last two words came out in a pained whisper.

"But I still want to know. Inside you, Bucky, does it really work? I've watched you for four years, and"—she hesitated—"loved you for most of the four. So just tell me. Is it all true?"

The features in her face softened, as she looked into his eyes. "Please."

Bucky remembered past moments when Sam and then Dan and Miss Cochran had faced this exact same crossroads. And then girls such as Deirdre and Tracy had at least had a glimpse of the life Jesus offered, and turned away. But nobody had ever meant to him what Lisa did. Sitting there in the moonlight, the weight of such a destiny in her eyes—he winced. Something inside him cried out for Lisa to choose.

"Yes, it is," he told her, his voice husky. "It sure is."

"It's what I want to do then."

He felt something catch in his throat. "Are you sure?"

Lisa nodded. "Yes."

Not knowing why, he slipped an arm around her and pulled her closer as a kind of Sabbath joy flooded him. "You know something? I'd rather . . . have you do this than to get you back." He looked up at the stars as if to send up a message of thanks. "I mean it."

She gave him a tiny smile. "How would you feel about getting both?"

A soft shuffling sound made them both look up. A tall figure was approaching in the darkness, and Bucky felt a momentary flutter of apprehension.

"Stone? Is that you?"

"Jeff?" Bucky half-rose off the concrete bench. "Man, what are you going here?"

The pitcher laughed. "Well, I was just coming through town on my way back home. So I called your house, and your mom gave me the number of . . ." He paused, turning to Lisa. "Sorry, what's your name again?"

"Lisa."

"Yeah. Your house. And then your mom said you guys were probably down here. Hope you don't think I was spying or something."

"No way." Bucky slid over to make room, but Jeff casually parked himself on the sidewalk right next to the couple. "So what's up?"

"Well, we just got word of the playoff schedule this afternoon at school. Varsity, I mean. Final game's going to be on a Friday night after all."

"For sure?"

"Yeah." Jeff shook his head. "Sorry. I mean, I guess there's a better-than-decent chance that's going to affect you. From the way you and Litton are playing and your team's doing."

"If it happens, it happens."

The player from Davis leaned forward. "There's no way you guys would play? I mean, *the* final game of your whole high school career?"

"Nope." Bucky was adamant. "Not on Sabbath."

"Man, that's heavy." Jeff seemed impressed. "Anyway, sorry to kind of rain on . . ." He glanced around at the darkness. "I guess it's your Sabbath right now, isn't it?"

"Uh huh."

Jeff laughed. "I guess cuddling on a park bench is allowed then?"

"You wouldn't believe it if I told you what we were actually doing." Bucky was suddenly sober.

"What?"

Bucky turned to Lisa. "You tell him, babe."

She reddened, her hand tightening in Bucky's. "I . . . just decided to become a Christian again."

Their visitor let out a yell. "Whoa! Are you kidding?"

"No. Just about two minutes ago." She gave a little laugh, then suddenly grew emotional. "Sorry. I've been crying so much lately, and now I just get all weepy over the least little thing."

"This isn't the least little thing." Jeff, bubbling with enthusiasm, came over and gave Lisa a huge hug. "Praise the Lord! That's fantastic news."

The trio visited another few minutes, and then began walking back out to the main sidewalk where Jeff had parked his car. "So what are you going to do now?" he asked.

"What do you mean?"

"Well, you know, you're a Christian now. So what next?"

Lisa turned and faced the two ballplayers. "Do you know what I want to do?"

"What?" It was Bucky who asked.

"Get baptized."

He felt a renewed sense of sheer happiness. "Babe, that's so great. I can't wait."

"No, I mean like right now. Tonight."

"Go for it." Jeff pumped both fists in the air and then pounded them on the hood of his car.

"Wait a minute," Bucky put in. "Tonight?"

"Why not?" she asked. "I want to right now."

"I know, but . . ." It was such an odd thought he didn't know what to say.

"Hey." Jeff began pacing back and forth in front of his battered Ford. "When Philip met that Ethiopian guy in the chariot, they had that Bible study and then he got baptized right there. Same day, man." He flashed Lisa an ebullient grin. "Why wait?"

"Yeah, but . . ." Bucky hesitated. "Are you going to be baptized as a . . . an Adventist? Or . . . what?"

"I want to be what you are," she told him simply. "I want to be an Adventist like you."

"Fantastic," Jeff murmured again.

"Yeah, but, babe, you haven't studied all that stuff."

"Yes, I have." She thrust both hands in her jacket pockets and looked up at him defiantly. "When you were studying with Dan, I heard a whole bunch of it. And then when I moved, you gave me that extra set of Bible lessons. Remember?"

Bucky had forgotten that part. "So?"

"So when I got to Seattle, I went through every single one of them."

"Lisa . . ."

"And I know it's all true." She looked at Jeff and then back to Bucky. "I want to be baptized."

CHAPTER 11

THE BEST BAPTISM

"What's this about, Bucky?"

He grinned to himself. "I really can't tell you. But it's kind of a good emergency. Can you meet us over at the church?"

A pause on the other end of the line. "Well, I can guarantee you I'm not wearing my Sabbath suit at the moment." Pastor Jensen's sense of humor still showed through even at 10:00 on a Friday night. "But if you want me to come, I'll come."

"You won't be sorry," Bucky promised him. "We'll see you there in a few minutes."

He hit the off button and handed the cellular phone back to Jeff. "You're comin' too, right?"

"Wouldn't miss it, brother." Jeff peeked at his watch. "We better get a move on."

Just as Bucky and Lisa were climbing into the back seat, he thought of something. "Can I borrow the phone again? I ought to call Dan."

Fifteen minutes later they pulled into the parking lot of the Seventh-day Adventist church. Pastor Jensen's car was already in the reserved staff slot, and Bucky could see Dan's Camaro just pulling in from the other side. "Looks like the gang's all here," he murmured to Lisa, squeezing her hand.

The silver-haired pastor climbed out of his car, adjusting his rumpled sweatshirt. "Hi, folks." He squinted through his glasses at Lisa. "You look awfully familiar, young lady."

"Pastor Jensen, this is Lisa Nichols. You remember her from a couple of years ago."

"Of course!" He pumped her hand enthusiastically. "Bucky had told me you were back in town. What a delight to see you again!"

"And this is Jeff. He goes to Calvary Church up in Sacramento, and we're friends from baseball."

"Jeff." Pastor Jensen shook his hand as well. "Listen, please give my regards to your associate pastor. Mike Corvallis, right? I attended a Holy Spirit training seminar he put on about a year ago."

"Sure." Jeff grinned.

"Well, let's go inside and you can dispel the mystery." The pastor greeted Dan and Julie as well. "We may as well have a Young Adults meeting here. Looks like we've got a quorum."

He disarmed the alarm system and turned on some lights as the five teenagers filed into the back of the church. "Not bad," Jeff commented, surveying the sanctuary.

"OK then." Pastor Jensen sat down a row ahead of the students and turned in the pew to face them. "Like I told you, Bucky, this better be good."

"Well, I think it is," he responded. "We're here for a baptism."

The pastor thought a moment, then grinned. "I guess that must be you . . . or you . . . or you." He glanced from Lisa to Julie to Jeff. "'Cause I've already got Dan and Bucky." They all laughed.

"It's me." Lisa, a bit embarrassed, raised her hand. "I want to be baptized."

"Tonight," Jeff put in.

"Tonight?" The pastor's eyes widened in surprise.

"Uh huh."

"Tonight?" he repeated.

"Like that Ethiopian guy," Jeff interjected. "Like he said, 'What's to prevent us from going for it?'"

Pastor Jensen scratched at his stubbly chin. "Well, Lisa, of course I'm thrilled. Some of us have been praying for you the whole last two and a half years."

"I know," she said softly. "I got your Christmas cards."

"And you're sure you know what you're doing?"

"Yes." It was a simple statement. "I've given my heart to God, and I want to have the same kind of experience that Bucky's had."

"Well, if you're baptized here in this church—by me—then you're being baptized as a Seventh-day Adventist Christian. Which means you understand and accept the special truths we believe God has blessed us with. Are you . . . in that situation?"

"Pastor J, she knows all that stuff," Bucky cut in. "When I studied with Dan, she listened to a whole lot of it. Plus she did the lessons herself, which I didn't know until tonight."

He shook his head, pleased. "It's wonderful how God works." Then he turned to Lisa. "But I want to hear it from you. I'm not going to quiz you here in front of your friends, but let me ask you in a very straightforward way: do you understand and accept the gospel message?"

Her face glowed. "Yes, I do."

"And you've accepted Jesus as your own personal Saviour?"

She nodded.

"And you have confidence in our Adventist perspectives on the truths of the Christian faith?"

"Uh huh."

The pastor's voice seemed almost a bit choked as he responded. "Well, Lisa, it would be my great honor to baptize you into the family of God."

A thrill shot through Bucky, and he put an arm around his girlfriend. "All right!" Jeff, on the other side, gave her a thumbs-up gesture.

"But now, folks, let me just do a bit of campaigning myself." The older man put both hands on the back of the pew. "Two things. First of all, you caught me by surprise . . . and the baptistry isn't filled. So a baptism right now, this very minute, would be kind of hard."

"We don't mind waiting," Dan said.

"Well, sure. And if you want to do that, that's fine." He nodded in agreement. "But here's something else. Lisa wants to be baptized into this church. This church *family*. To me, it would be even more special if she could wait and do it when the whole family's here."

A bit of the excitement began to fade in Bucky's heart. "But . . . man, we don't want to wait. Do we?" He looked over at Lisa.

"No." She gulped. "Can't we do it now?"

"Well, I'm talking about tomorrow morning," Pastor Jensen told her. "Believe me, I don't want to dampen this beautiful enthusiasm. We could just come right back here in the morning, with your families and friends and the whole congregation. It's just a few hours from now."

Lisa thought for a moment. "What do you think, Bucky?"

He shook his head. "Babe, it's totally up to you. Whatever you want."

"Jeff?" The tall senior chewed on a fingernail, thinking. "I agree with what your pastor said. It's great to have the whole body of Christ here. But . . . it's kind of special just with all us kids too, I gotta admit."

"Why don't you wait?" Dan suggested. "I mean, that gives you a chance to tell your mom and stuff. Who knows, maybe she'll come."

That seemed to make sense. At last Lisa gave a little nod.

"What about you, Hilliard?" Bucky interjected. "Man, we want you here." All at once he gave the athlete a little nudge. "Look, just come stay at my place. Then you can worship with us in the morning and be with Lisa when she's baptized. Would that work?"

He shrugged. "I think so. I can call my mom and tell her."

"Is it a deal then?" The white-haired pastor climbed to his feet. "I better give our head deacon a call and get the water flowing around here." He laughed. "This is the kind of emergency we just love."

A festive mood hung in the air the next morning around the breakfast table. Jeff, wearing some borrowed dress clothes of Bucky's, raved about the strawberry blintzes and waffles Mom had prepared. "Man, Stone, if you Adventists eat like this every Saturday, I could go for it real quick."

The church seemed especially full that morning as Bucky glanced around. Dan and Julie were both there, along with Miss Cochran. Lisa, of course, with her mom, who glanced around at the unfamiliar surroundings with a look of quizzical nervousness written on her face. And about halfway through Sabbath school, Sam walked in and sat down on the other side of Rachel Marie.

"Man, how'd you get here?" Bucky grinned his approval.

"Dan called me early this morning. So I borrowed my roommate's car."

"That's great."

At the appointed moment, Pastor Jensen slowly entered the baptismal tank and held out his hand for Lisa. Bucky felt something tighten in his throat. The senior girl had never looked so beautiful as she did right at that moment in her plain white robe.

"Folks," the pastor began, "I have to open my heart to you right here. This is one of the happiest days I can remember in my ministry." Briefly he related how the five young people had come to him in the darkness of a Friday night. "But they decided to wait until today, so that you could all join us."

"And Bucky," he went on, "we're starting to lose count of how many precious people have come to know Jesus through your witness." He glanced down at Lisa. "But I know Dan and Sam won't mind if I make a guess that this is probably your favorite one." He looked over at the tall athlete. "Come on up here, Bucky. I know Lisa wants you close." He smiled. "In fact, Dan, you come up here too. Julie? Jeff? Sam? Sheila? You're their teacher. And Mrs. Nichols, you come too. What a wonderful thing to have good parents support their children."

As the group grew larger around the baptismal tank, the pastor suddenly laughed. "You know, folks, it's such a crowd here, why don't you all come up? We've been waiting three years for this moment, and I don't think the fire marshal will mind. Please, if you join us in celebrating with heaven today, just come forward and stand as close as you can."

Even though the platform was filled with people, Bucky still managed to catch Lisa's glance just before Pastor Jensen immersed her beneath the surface. Tears filled his eyes as he remembered all the prayers, the times of doubt.

He'd waited so long for this moment . . . and now God had come through. Jeff noticed Bucky's emotion and put an arm around his friend.

Someone in the back of the group spontaneously began to sing "Blest Be the Tie That Binds" as Lisa came out of the water. Bucky tried to sing, but it was too much for him. Lisa gave the pastor a quick hug, and then began to climb the steps. Still dripping wet, she came to Bucky and threw her arms around his neck.

"I love you," she whispered. "Thanks, babe, for waiting for me." He held her tight, the sudden dampness of his clothes mingling with something close to pure joy.

"I assume the whole world is coming over for lunch," Mom murmured in his ear as she gave Lisa a kiss.

"Yeah." He couldn't help but grin. "However many we can fit in."

After church, Mrs. Nichols excused herself, but everyone else did come over, including Jeff. "I'll just take some more of what you guys had for breakfast," he laughed.

It was a great Sabbath afternoon, just lounging on the thick carpeting in the Stones' living room. Lisa kept snuggling up next to Bucky, rapturously gazing at him until Dan threw a sofa pillow at both of them.

"And you, Hilliard," he announced, "can just count on one thing. Stone and me are going to kick your tail clear over into Nevada the next time we meet on the ball diamond. I'm going to personally raise your ERA about 45 points all by myself."

"That's right," Bucky agreed, giving Lisa another squeeze. "He's making it a matter of personal prayer."

The days of spring dropped into place as the seniors began their official "Fifty-Day Countdown to Graduation."

And the Litton/Stone baseball duo continued at such a hot pace that the local newspaper even commented on it.

"Coach Demerest knows who carries the big bats for this town," concluded one sports reporter. "Both times Messrs. Litton and Stone have absented themselves—always for religious reasons—the Panthers have come up short. And now with the baseball playoffs in just one week, Hampton Beach has got to be wondering: will this team have to play a final Friday evening playoff game without its two fearsome weapons?"

"I don't get it," Bucky muttered to Dan after their next-to-last practice session. "I mean, I know we're hitting good. Almost over our heads, in fact. But the way the team lost both those Friday night games, it's almost like God is setting us up for something."

"Yeah. Kind of weird." In both of the Friday night contests the Panthers had hit well. But in the first game, three errors and a bad call at home plate had cost the team the victory. And in the second game, a home contest at Hampton Beach, the two players taking Bucky and Dan's spots had performed abysmally, going a combined zero for nine at the plate.

Right before the final game of the regular varsity season, Coach Demerest called the two outfielders into his office for one last visit. "Everything still the same?" He didn't have to spell out what the question was.

"Yeah." Dan nodded, staring intently at his shoes.

"Fellows, I don't know what to say," the older man said. "But I just don't think we can win without you. Not in a championship game, and not against those guys from Davis—which it's almost for sure going to be. And not against Hilliard, who already skunked us once." He looked from one to the other. "Now, I'm not going to belabor all the variables. You men have your religion 'thing'—and I respect it. On the other hand, if we get to the finals, it'll be your last game ever at this level. And you have a team that needs you. How you weigh those two things is strictly up to you, and I'm not going to push you either way. But I want you to have all of that—both sides—in your mind as you consider your decision."

"Coach, we already know what we have to do," Bucky said softly. "I'm sorry."

The athletic director looked at him evenly. "That's it?"

"Yeah." Dan gave a little shrug. "We got no choice, Coach."

"Well, you *do* have a choice," the older man snapped. "But . . . I'm not going to comment on that."

Bucky gulped. "Coach, there's no way that game can be moved?"

"No way." His face tightened. "District says no way, and I say no way too. We play our games as they come assigned to us."

The last regular-season game turned out to be a laugher for the home team. Bucky and Dan seemed to come up with the bases full of Panthers every single time, and they combined to drive in a total of eight runs. Back-to-back-to-back homers with the catcher, Anthony, brought the capacity crowd to its feet in the seventh inning as the three long balls stretched the score to an embarrassing 12-1 blowout.

"Fifteen and five. Not bad." Bucky walked around the locker room, giving high fives to every single member of the squad. "Good going, you guys."

One of the infielders gave him a pained look. "Man, Stone, it stinks playing those two playoff games knowing we'll just crash and burn Friday no matter what."

"Yeah," the pitcher chimed in. "We're dead meat without you and Litton."

"What do you want me to do?" Bucky grimaced. "You know I can't play."

Anthony, still glowing from his big home run, came over and stood beside Bucky. "The man can't play and you know it."

Sabbath after church he and Dan talked about it while Julie and Lisa spread out their picnic lunch at the lake. "When does Friday's game start?" Dan asked him.

"I guess it's at 6:00 instead of at 7:00 like the others. I don't know why."

"So we could go and play the first couple innings," Dan told him.

His friend frowned. "Man, Litton, that's dangerous stuff. Leaving after two innings? What if someone gets hurt like last time? Then everybody starts screaming at you to play. 'Course, they're going to do that anyway."

"I don't know." Dan reached out and grabbed a cookie out of the bowl. "Guys on the team this year seem to know where we're coming from. Actually, I kind of think they almost . . . I don't know, support us."

Bucky nodded. "You know, it almost seems that way." He remembered what Anthony had said in the locker room.

"May not be an issue even," Dan told him. "After all our what-iffing, Stone, we might get beat on Monday."

"No way." He waved at the girls. "With cheerleaders like these?"

And after Monday evening's contest, it certainly did look as if the Panthers had a rendezvous with destiny. Bucky pounded out three hits and played spectacular defense in the outfield, making a circus catch over the fence to bring back what would otherwise have been a game-tying two-run homer. And Dan's two doubles pushed his average up above .450, leading the district. The two senior girls went out with them to celebrate the 10-7 triumph. "Jeff's game is

tomorrow," Dan told the others as they enjoyed the cama-
raderie at the ice-cream parlor. "Think we should go?"

"Up to Davis, right?"

Mr. Willis had given Bucky the week off from work, so
the foursome did make the drive up I-80 to see the Devils
in their playoff opener. And Jeff was true to form, allowing
only two runs in a complete-game performance.

"Can you pitch again Friday?" Bucky asked him after
the game as the group met in the parking lot.

"That's the plan. Morales goes in Round Two, and then
if we win that one, I guess I'll be back on Friday."

"Your arm's OK?" Dan asked.

"Sure."

"I'm sorry to hear that," he laughed. "Why isn't God answering our prayers?" They wished the pitcher the best of
luck before pulling back out onto the freeway.

Wednesday afternoon before government class Dan
slapped a newspaper column down on Bucky's desk. "One
of the kids just gave me this."

"What is it?"

"Read."

A sports columnist for the Sacramento *Bee* had pieced
together a story about the burgeoning friendship between
Bucky and Jeff Hilliard. "Are these two athletes, now spiritual soulmates, destined to meet again on a baseball field?"
the writer queried. "Or will superstar slugger Bucky Stone
again defer because of his religious faith? If the Devils and
Panthers both win tonight, the East Bay will get answers to
both of those questions."

There *was* a special intensity to night games, Bucky decided, as he and Dan trotted out to their positions that
evening. The stands were packed with Hampton Beach
students and a large contingent of adult fans as the
Panthers again rolled to a win under the lights. Pleasant

Hill tried to come back in the late innings, but Bucky and Dan keyed a four-run rally in the sixth to ice the victory. Over in the corner of the dugout they saw Coach Demerest talking on a cellular phone.

"It's Davis," he told them afterward. "I guess they clobbered Vallejo by about eight runs."

Bucky felt a twinge of frustration. So it *would* be Jeff Hilliard going for the trophy on Friday night.

"Coach, we've been thinking," he said. "The game's at 6:00, right?"

"Yeah." Demerest put the phone away in his duffel bag. "It's earlier so TV people can get scores onto the 10:00 news. All of northern California does it that way, they tell me."

"And it's a home game for us, right?"

"Yeah. We were 15-5 and they were 14-6."

"Well, look. Dan and I can play until 7:00."

"What are you talking about?"

"Sundown's at 7:20," Bucky told him. "We could play the first couple innings. Maybe even three."

The crowd was milling around outside the dugout area, and the coach moved a bit closer so he could hear them more easily. "Are you sure?"

"Yeah. But . . . for sure by then, we'd have to go." He took a deep breath. "No matter what the circumstances, or if we're behind or ahead or . . . anything."

"Yeah, Coach." Dan nodded his agreement. "Who knows, we might be able to knock in at least a couple runs by then."

"I don't know what the team would think," Demerest told them. "Playing my ringers for just the first little bit and then you take off? Come on."

"You could at least ask them."

At last the coach gave a little nod. "I guess. The way you're swinging the bats, we'd take anything we could get."

CHAPTER 12

"WE'RE NOT PLAYING"

It was hard to concentrate Friday morning during classes. Everyone at Hampton Beach High School was planning to be at the big varsity final that evening, and even the teachers seemed to be infected by playoff fever. Mr. Rojas spent the entire period reminiscing about a Dodger-Yankee World Series game his dad had taken him to when he was just a kid—and how that proved the United States of America had a wonderful government.

With all of the emotional ups and downs in the past few weeks, Bucky didn't know if he could even face the three innings he was hoping to play. After so much media buzz, what if he messed up? And then he would have to face that moment when he and Dan had to leave the playing field . . . in front of hundreds of fans. What if the Panthers were down by a run? And then what if his team lost, after four years of building for this one critical contest?

He felt buoyed up a bit by a phone call he'd received

that morning during breakfast. "Just wanted to let you know I'm thinking of you men and praying for you," Pastor Jensen told him. "Your testimony for Jesus is a very precious thing to our church family, and we're awfully proud of you."

Just as school let out, Lisa approached him in the parking lot. "Did you see this?" she asked, waving a copy of *Highlights,* the school newspaper.

"Huh uh. What is it?"

"There's something about you and Dan."

Taking the student newspaper, he leaned against the Toyota to read. In the editor's box was a large headline: "Waiting for the Moment."

"Did Tracy write this?" For some reason he'd seen little of the redhead genius the past semester.

"Yeah. I think it's good."

He read through the brief editorial, feeling a stir of memories from last year. "Some students want this playoff game moved," she had written. "After four years of waiting, they say, Bucky Stone and Dan Litton should have their chance at a varsity baseball trophy. And who could argue with that sentiment?"

But then the editorial went on. "I'm glad they're not moving the game! Because tonight at about 7:00 p.m. we'll have the opportunity to witness something rare. As the sun sets this evening, two high school seniors—*our* fellow seniors—will pick up their mitts and their batting gloves and depart from the baseball field and the game we know they love. With a baseball *final* still in progress, they'll drive away from Hampton High and into their Sabbath, leaving behind a team they're extremely loyal to . . . because they're answering tonight to a higher Loyalty. There's Team—and there's Country—and then there's God. And tonight a couple of unique men will show our high school, a huge contingent from Davis, a row of sports reporters, and a watching Bay Area what priorities are all about."

Bucky shook his head slowly. "Wow."

"Read the rest of it," Lisa urged.

There was one more paragraph. "Maybe you don't understand what motivates them. 'We don't get it,' we say. But perhaps that's because some of us never looked hard enough or deep enough. All we can see is a championship. Sure, we want that big silver cup. And even without the Panthers' two big bats, we might still get it. But, speaking for just this one reporter, I wouldn't trade tonight's 7:00 p.m. moment for a championship . . . or for 50 of them."

He carefully folded the newspaper and slipped it into his notebook. "Did very many of the kids see this?"

"It's all over the place," Lisa responded. "Everyone in the hallway was talking about it."

Pregame practice was a short, tense affair, with Coach Demerest wordlessly motioning them through quick drills in the field. Bucky breathed a silent prayer as he finished batting practice. "I might only get one at-bat," he whispered. "Please, Lord, help make it count. Everybody's watching tonight."

The Davis team bus pulled into the parking lot right on schedule, and the Devils poured out, bouncing around their coach in eager little steps. "There's Hilliard," Dan observed. "Wonder how he's feeling?"

"Nervous, just like us," Bucky grinned. "Come on, let's go say hi."

The three athletes had only a quick moment together before the Devil's coach whistled them onto the playing field for their allotted warm-up time. The two Panther members rejoined their own team in the locker room for a last-minute huddle.

"Well, men, this is what we've prepared for," Coach

Demerest told them. "And I know this is a unique kind of evening with our shuffled lineup. But hopefully we can grab an early lead and then hang on." He glanced around. "I'm proud of each of you players. Win or lose, we had a terrific season."

"Forget that win-or-lose stuff, Coach," one of the relief pitchers said. "Let's win!"

Dan and Bucky retreated to a corner of the dressing room just before 6:00. It suddenly hit the younger player that the three quick innings were going to be their final game together. "Man, Litton, this is it," he said, feeling a flood of nostalgia. He and Dan had been through so much.

"Don't go weepy on me, Stone." Then Dan himself had to blink hard. "That's heavy, though. We've played a lot of games together."

Bucky could feel his other teammates' eyes on him as he and Dan prayed. "Lord, please bless this team," he said softly. "Whether they win or lose . . . we can't ask You for that. But please touch the hearts of every single player, because these guys are really special."

"And be with Jeff," Dan added. "We want to play hard against him, but he's our brother. Protect and bless him tonight. And in whatever his future is."

They opened their eyes to see Coach Demerest waiting for them. "Ready?"

"Yeah." Blushing, Bucky picked up his glove. "We're all set."

"Give me something good. And quick," the athletic director muttered as the two outfielders went by him.

A huge roar went up from the crowd as the PA announced the starting lineup. "And in right field, Number Seven, Bucky Stone." Bucky could see dozens of copies of *Highlights* in the grandstands as he trotted past the crowd and out into right field. "Tracy must have run off extras for the whole town to read," he muttered to Dan before taking his position.

The Panthers' ace pitcher, Dennis, was a tall Black senior with a wicked slider. He mowed down the first three hitters on a total of 11 pitches, and trotted with his team into the dugout with two strikeouts already under his belt.

"Way to grab those K's," Bucky praised him as he picked out a bat. "Come on, you guys, let's get some runs." He watched from the far end of the dugout as Jeff Hilliard took his eight warmup pitches. The strikes were whistling in with a vicious *pop!* as they hit the catcher's mitt.

"He looks intense," Dan grunted. "Let's get 'im!"

The first batter popped up weakly, but the second baseman managed to squeeze one through the hole between third and short. Bucky climbed into the batter's box and gave his friend on the mound a nervous grin. It was against playoff protocol to converse with the opposite team, and he really had too many butterflies to call out anything very friendly, even to a fellow Christian.

"Help me to do my best, Lord," he whispered. Mentally he traveled back to Tuesday's Round One game up in Davis. Jeff was clever at mixing up his pitches and not getting into a predictable pattern, but Bucky and Dan had both noticed how the Devils' pitcher had a slider that tailed away from righthanders—and out of the strike zone. "We got to stay away from those," Dan had surmised. "Don't swing at them if they're outside."

As he waved the bat back and forth now, waiting, he rehearsed that thought. "Watch the outside slider. On the other hand, if it's up in the strike zone and you can go to right field with it . . ."

The first two pitches were exactly as predicted, low and outside. They looked good as Jeff released them, but Bucky could tell from the ball's rotation that they were going to spin out. "Hit me in, Stone," the runner at first hollered out. "This guy's no pitcher."

The next pitch was a hard fastball, just on the outside of the plate. With a short, smooth swing, he sent the pitch rocketing right over the second baseman's head and into right-center field. The baserunner on first made it clear around to third on the long single.

The Panthers erupted into cheers as the crowd buzzed its approval. "First and third, only one out!"

Dan walked up to the plate, relishing his role as cleanup hitter. "Come on, Litton. Big stick now," Bucky exhorted him. And Jeff, worried about falling behind in the count, didn't bother with the low-and-outside stuff. His second pitch was a curve ball that didn't break enough, and Dan jumped on it for a smash single up the middle. The run scored, and moments later Bucky also came in from third to score when Anthony put a sacrifice fly deep on the warning track.

"Good job! Good job! We need those two runs!" Coach Demerest barked out his approval. "Now hold 'em!"

Both teams went down in order in the second, and the crowd's enthusiasm was stilled somewhat when the Devils' first baseman unloaded on a 2-0 pitch from Dennis in the third. The home run narrowed the game to a nail-biting 2-1 lead.

Bucky glanced at his watch as the team took their places in the dugout. "Six fifty-three." His stomach tightened. "Litton, we can bat right now and then we've got to split."

"Yeah." Dan's grip tightened on the metal bat. "Last call for heroes."

The first batter patiently worked the count to a full 3-2, fouled off two pitches, and finally watched as ball four was just a bit high. "Yeah! Good eye!" Bucky pumped his fist in satisfaction as the second baseman trotted down to first.

"This is it, Lord. Last chance."

The opposing team, realizing that Bucky and Dan were the big guns, were playing deep at the corners. Both Bucky and Dan were capable of smashing a line drive in either direction, and infielders throughout the district were a bit intimidated, especially in a big final game like this one. A tempting thought crept into Bucky's mind as he took the first pitch for ball one.

Should I try it? The next pitch was right down the middle. Dumping a bunt down the third-base line he sprinted madly toward first. Jeff, who had come off the mound to the wrong side, had no chance to get the little squib roller, and the third baseman was way too deep to make a play. He fielded the ball bare-handed and threw desperately to first, but Bucky had already crossed the bag.

"Yeah! Heads up!" Coach Demerest was hollering with the rest of the team. "Surprise, surprise!"

Dan, grinning his approval, stepped into the batter's box and waved the bat menacingly. Jeff stared down the 60-foot-6-inch corridor toward home plate as though he'd never met the two young Christians, his face a mask of concentration.

It was a power-versus-power confrontation, and Bucky rubbed his hands together over at first base, relishing the moment. He and Dan would be leaving the game in a moment, but what a perfect ending. The stocky slugger let a ball and a strike go by, and stepped out to rub some dirt on his hands. In the stands, Bucky could see Julie and Lisa jumping up and down. "Come on, Litton," he muttered. "Right now, baby. Right now."

The next pitch was a hard fastball, and Dan was ready. He slammed the ball deep into left field, and the fielder never even turned around to pursue it. It was gone the moment it left the bat. A huge roar went up from the crowd as Dan trotted around the bases just behind Bucky. There was a three-way round of high-fives at home plate as they watched the scoreboard runs total jump up to a big five. The PA system rumbled enthusiastically with a drum roll and synthesized horn fanfare.

"Way to go, Litton!" Bucky gave Dan a half-embrace as the big center fielder waved to the crowd. "Way to end the year."

They waded through the mob-like reception in the dugout, and sank down on the bench. It was time to start gathering up their things. For a moment, Bucky glanced around for Anthony, who was supposed to bat next. But the catcher was still standing at the entrance to the dugout. "You better get up there," he told him.

The other player shook his head. "No, I'm going to wait."

Bucky swallowed at a lump in his throat as he and Dan picked up their athletic duffel bags. "Good luck, you guys," he said, shaking hands with several of them. The break in the game was a bit strange, as though someone had hit the pause button on a VCR.

"Way to come through." Coach Demerest shook hands with Bucky and Dan. "No matter what happens now, you guys are champs."

As Bucky and Dan exited from the dugout, a new round of applause began to build in the stands. Embarrassed, Bucky gave a little wave to the many hometown fans. All at once, the PA system crackled. "Ladies and gentlemen, let's hear it for Panther stars Bucky Stone and Dan Litton, who have to leave the game. Thanks, men, for four great years of athletic excellence for Hampton Beach High School!"

Bucky looked around, confused. *What's going on?* Apparently most of the people in the stands had read Tracy's article in the student newspaper, because now many of them were rising to their feet. Bucky could see Jeff standing on the pitcher's mound, clapping with the others.

A lump came into Bucky's throat as the applause grew to a roar. Overcome, he raised his hand in the air, pointing toward the sky with a final wordless testimony. The umpire stood at home plate, confused by the delay.

"We better go," Dan managed, a bit choked up himself. "But man, this is something else."

All at once they heard a stir in the dugout as Anthony and the other players on the team filed onto the playing field. Bucky watched, mystified, as the chunky catcher went over to the home-plate umpire and said something. The blue-clad official shook his head for a moment, then pulled off his mask and came striding over toward the dugout.

"Demerest, what is this?" he demanded. "These guys say they're not going to play now."

"What?"

"That's what your kid tells me."

"What's going on, Anthony?" A bit of red crept into the athletic director's face.

"We're not playin'," the catcher told him. "Not without Litton and Stone."

"You sure are playing," the older man retorted quickly, adding a short profanity. "They've got to go, and I can't fix that. We've been all through it. But we've got a game to play here and a four-run lead, and we're gonna play. Now put on a helmet and get up there."

"No." The catcher put his hands on his hips. "Litton and Stone are part of the team. We're going to finish the game with them."

"They can't play." Now Demerest's voice was rising.

"Then we'll wait until they *can* play," the player retorted, matching the coach's vehemence. "These guys believe in God, man. And they can't play now. So get with the umpire here and move the game. Let's finish it next week."

"I don't do business that way," the older man retorted. "Plus the district office would never let us."

"Fine." Anthony dropped his batting helmet in the dirt and crossed his arms. "I'm not hitting, and neither is anyone else on the team. You see if you can beat these guys all by yourself, Coach."

What's going on? Bucky wondered again. He and Dan had no idea something like this might have been brewing. How long had Anthony and the other guys been thinking about it? All three of the visiting outfielders had come trotting in to second base to see what was going on.

The umpire edged closer. "Demerest, get your guys under control or this game is over," he snapped. "This is ridiculous."

The Panthers' coach pushed a finger in Anthony's chest. "You heard the man. Get up to hit now or we forfeit. Is that what you want? To kiss goodbye a 5-1 lead in the varsity finals because of some stupid . . . religious debate?"

"It's not stupid!" Now Anthony's voice had risen until many of the fans could hear him. "Litton and Stone are the best guys on this team and you know it. They're Christians, man. They're the best guys in the school, even. And they shouldn't have to dump their last game, the *finals,* because you and the stupid office don't have brains enough to move the game. It's a *game,* Coach! Just move it!"

"No!" Now the coach and the indignant player were just inches away, staring at each other.

"One minute, Demerest," the umpire growled. "Sixty seconds from now this game goes to Davis."

"Hang on before you do that." A new voice entered the fray.

Bucky and Dan and the small knot of players turned to face Jeff Hilliard. "Now what?" the umpire demanded.

"These guys can't forfeit," the visiting pitcher told them.

"Because we're not going to play tonight either."

It took a minute for the announcement to sink in. "What in the world are you talking about?" The home-plate official was clearly confused and upset.

"Hampton's walking out," Jeff told him, his voice calm. "And so are we." He took a deep breath. "I just talked to some of our guys, and we're not going to play any more tonight. We want to play the Panthers, *with* Litton and Stone . . . or nothing."

"You guys are nuts." The umpire looked from one dugout to the other. "I'm in charge here, and I'm telling you, this game goes on right now. In one minute. In *half* a minute. And the first team that doesn't show, they lose. This is ridiculous!"

"Well, look around you." Jeff was still calm, but he towered over the angry umpire. "They're not playing; *we're* not playing. Who are you going to forfeit the game to?"

"What's the matter with you? You're down four runs and might get a free forfeit. And you're going to turn it down?"

Now several of the Devils came up and stood next to Jeff. "What kind of championship trophy would that be for us?" he said quietly. "From a forfeit? We want to play these guys at full strength." Then he took a step forward. "Anyway, a man's religious faith is way more important than this ballgame. All of us . . . on the other team, even . . . we've got to support that."

The sun was nearly gone from the horizon now, as the umpire's shoulders sagged. "What the . . ." He turned toward Coach Demerest. "Any bright ideas?" he asked dourly.

"The district commissioner is right over there," Jeff added politely. "Why don't you just ask him? We can all play Monday if the Panthers are willing."

Tension was still thick as the game official stood there in the twilight, considering. At last he shook his head and turned toward the grandstands. There was a long, almost surreal pause as the entire crowd sat in complete silence. The subdued conversation went on between the two men for several minutes, and Bucky could see both men shaking their heads in frustration.

All at once the PA system crackled again. "Ladies and gentlemen, we thank you for your patience. Due to . . ." There followed an odd moment of confused silence. "Due to unusual circumstances, the remainder of this game is being postponed. At 7:00 p.m. Monday we'll resume this district varsity final competition right here on this field between the Davis Devils and your own Hampton Beach High School Panthers."

A burst of applause began to race around the infield as the crowd stood to its feet and started clapping. Then the announcer, with a bit of humor showing through in his voice, added: "And we get to keep our four-run lead over the weekend!"

ENDINGS AND
BEGINNINGS

Bucky spent the Sabbath in a kind of suspended disbe-lief. How could his spiritual journey at Hampton Beach High School have possibly come to such a dramatic con-clusion? A threatened double forfeit, with both teams re-fusing to play a final game? Several sports reporters had followed him home to Woodman Avenue afterwards, and he and Lisa had spent a good half hour on his front porch answering their questions.

"So this is your . . . Sabbath right now?" one of them had queried.

Bucky nodded.

"That's a pretty high price you put on it then."

All four of the journalists waited to hear his response. "Well," he told them, "I remember my pastor telling me once, 'Calvary's the most important price ever paid for anything.' And if I'm that important to God, then honoring Him is that important to me."

It was just after sundown the next evening that he drove over to the other side of town. Having looked up Anthony's address in the phone book, he just had to find out something.

Kids all looking for something to do on a Saturday night crowded the three rows of apartment buildings. Several of them were pushing one another in a homemade cart, and they bumped carelessly into his Toyota as he parked.

"Watch it, you guys," he chided, but they had already rumbled down the street.

Carefully checking the slip of paper, he climbed the stairs to the third level and found the apartment number. A short, perspiring man answered the door. "Is Anthony home?"

He nodded. "Sure. Come in."

Anthony appeared at the entrance to the living room. "Hey, Stone. What's up?"

"Just came to see you."

"Come on back to my room."

The bulky catcher had a small bedroom in the rear of the apartment. "What brings you out here, man?"

Bucky sat down on the floor against a big Shaq Attack poster. "That was a heavy-duty thing you did last night."

The other player grinned. "Yeah. I can't believe we got away with it."

"How'd you know it was going to work?"

"I didn't, really. But . . . it was something we all had to do."

"I don't get it." Bucky leaned forward, a look of curiosity on his face. "So you and the other guys had already talked about it before the game?"

"Yeah. Well, not really until after we won on Wednesday. Up till then, we didn't know if it was going to even be a problem. 'Course, I always thought we would win."

"Well . . ." Bucky wasn't quite sure how to say what

he'd been wondering ever since the showdown at the ball-field. "If you guys were thinking of, you know, walking out like that . . ." He paused, trying to formulate his thought.

"What?"

"Don't get me wrong. It was the greatest thing anyone's ever done for me. And everybody's talking about it. But . . . if you guys were going to do that, why didn't you just tell Demerest ahead of time and push him to get the entire game moved?" Bucky gulped, feeling as if he hadn't said it very well.

"I talked to Dennis about that," Anthony admitted. "Telling the coach we didn't want to play without you and see if he'd arrange a switch."

"So?"

"Well, couple things. Someone said you and Litton had already asked him to switch it, and he said no way."

"That's true," Bucky admitted.

"And then—well, I gotta admit it. Most of the guys still weren't absolutely positive you and Litton would walk off the field. I mean, you skipped the two regular Friday night games and all. But in the finals? I remember Crook telling me, 'When it comes right down to the last game, Stone'll chicken out. He'll stay and play.' And then I asked him, 'If Litton and Stone leave, then will you hang with us on the walkout?' And he said sure."

Bucky felt a quiver in his stomach. So he and Dan had really been on trial with the Panthers and didn't even know it. "You guys are something else," he managed.

"Well, I gotta tell you this too."

"What?"

"If we'd been down in the game, I don't think we would have done it."

Bucky gave a slight shake of his head, confused. "I don't understand. How come?"

"Well, look. Let's say we're down. And then you and Litton leave. And all of a sudden, we pull this thing of 'Hey, we're walking off.' It'd look like some kind of desperation trick."

"But when we were up by four runs . . ."

"Yeah, then we could do it." Anthony grinned. "Because everyone knew we were the team to beat—we had the big lead. We probably would have won anyway. So it kind of gave us the . . ." He groped for a phrase.

"Some kind of, like, moral authority?"

"Yeah. Like that. We could do it with some class."

Bucky took a breath. "Well, all I know is, it was one unforgettable night. I owe you big-time, man."

"Let's just win Monday, Stone, and we'll be even."

Another thought popped into Bucky's mind. "But you had no idea that their pitcher, Hilliard, was going to jump in like that?"

"Oh, no way. I didn't know nothing about that." He laughed. "That was heavy, though. That poor ump just didn't have nowhere to go."

Sunday morning Bucky and Dan picked up Julie and Lisa, and they made the 45-minute drive up the interstate to Calvary Church. The praise band had just finished a high-energy worship segment when they spotted Jeff sitting near the front. "Hey, you guys! Who said you could come here?" He greeted Bucky with a teasing grin, then a hug. "This is great."

They spent the worship hour together without really getting a chance to talk. The crowds were slowly moving toward the exits before Bucky could ask his friend the same question. "What happened on Friday?"

Jeff looked away for a moment, gazing soberly at the huge cross at the front of the church. "Well, I knew you guys were leaving at sundown," he began slowly. "Which I think is the most awesome thing."

"I know, but that forfeit business . . ."

Jeff nodded. "I thought for a long time on Friday about stuff like that. Why should there be a game where somebody can't play just because of their beliefs? But I figured your own school had already wrestled with it and come up empty."

He went on. "But I did wonder if there was any way we could, you know, pitch in and try to get the game moved. Which we should have done. And I'd talked to about four of our guys, but didn't really pursue it." A pause. "But then when your guys walked out, a whole bunch of us over there by second base got into it again. And I said to them, 'Look, these guys are doing what we should be doing. You want to back them up?' And all of them said, 'Go for it.' "

"That's unreal," Dan put in. "All of them?"

"Well, a couple of them are Christians," Jeff told them. "And we'd talked about what you two guys believe. Plus, like we said the other night, who wants to win on a forfeit? 'Specially when you're down by four runs and probably were going to lose. That's really cheap."

Bucky nodded. "All I can say is this." He reached over and gave Jeff a grateful little poke in the shoulder. "What you did, and what Anthony did—that's the catcher on our team—man, Litton and I are never going to forget it." He felt Lisa's hand tighten in his.

"Hey, you guys are my brothers," Jeff asserted. "Even though you didn't treat me too good Friday." He kicked at Dan's ankle. "I gave you my best pitch and you hit it clean out of the ballpark."

⚾ ⚾ ⚾

It was a smaller crowd that reconvened at Hampton High's ballpark Monday evening. Some of the Davis supporters, knowing they were already down by four, hadn't made the trip, and the bleachers had scattered empty places.

But the game picked up right where it had been so abruptly paused—bottom of the third, no outs, 5-1 Panthers.

Jeff and Dennis, both having gotten three days to rest, resumed their pitching roles and shut out the opposing hitters until the final inning. In the top of the frame, Davis managed to load the bases with two outs. But the last hitter, swinging for the fences and a game-tying grand slam, got under the pitch and lofted an easy fly ball into right field. Calling Dan off, Bucky gloved the ball and held it aloft. Already on the pitcher's mound, Dennis, Anthony, and the infielders were beginning to celebrate. Hampton fans poured onto the field as Dan and Bucky trotted in to join the party.

"You hiding that ball?" Dan laughed.

"Yeah. The last out in the last game. I'm keeping this sucker."

Entering the free-for-all in the center of the diamond, Bucky gave high-fives to everyone in sight. He found Anthony and hugged him hard. "Thanks, man."

The catcher hesitated. "No, Stone. I gotta thank you. The way you and Litton did what you did . . . it got to me."

Bucky didn't know what to say. "Well, anyway, congratulations. We had a great season."

Even Coach Demerest had nothing but praise. "Good job, guys." He managed a smile. "Even if it took us three days to beat them!"

The celebration was still going on when Bucky peeled away and went across the long parking lot to where the Davis team bus was loading. Jeff, his athletic bag slung over his shoulder, was just climbing aboard. "Hey, Hilliard!"

The pitcher turned and came toward him. "Good job, Stone. You guys deserved the trophy."

Bucky shook his head. "Well, we both had good teams. Basically we got a lucky homer and that's all there was to it." He paused, remembering the hundreds of out-field plays and at-bats that make up four years of high school baseball competition. And then one quirky moment, one pitch that was a bit too good, one swing of the bat, meant you were a champion. It wasn't fair, but that's how the San Francisco *Chronicle's* sports report would see it the next day.

"You know," he said at last, "it's so dumb."

"What?"

"All of this. Baseball. And trophies." He looked directly at Jeff. "You and I are Christians. We know the stuff that really counts." A wave of emotion hit him and he had to struggle to get the words out. "The way you stood up for Dan and me and supported us . . . and then praying with us before games . . ."

Jeff nodded, moving a step closer. "Yeah. And then you guys walking off the field in order to be obedient to your beliefs." He paused. "I'm going to study this Sabbath business, Stone. I mean that."

The two athletes moved away from the bus and had a final prayer together.

The last three weeks of school were a frantic round of senior activities and cramming for finals. The prom was a huge Friday night bash, and Bucky and his three friends took some easy kidding about skipping it. "Sure, a ball game, Stone," one of the other athletes teased. "That's no big deal. But missing the prom? That's where all the female lips are going to be parked."

"Not all of them," the tall senior laughed, looking over at Lisa.

And then at last came the biggest Thursday of them all and graduation night. Bucky had attended the event all three previous times, but there was something especially giddy about finally putting on the cap and gown. Lisa helped him adjust his mortarboard and dangle the tassel just right.

"So you just missed the top GPA spot," she teased. "Little Tracy Givenchy beat you."

"Pretty hard to top a 4.0," he grumped, pretending to scowl.

"What'd you come in? Third?"

"No, fourth."

"How about Dan?"

He tried to look thoughtful. "I think he came in nine hundred and fortieth . . . but it might not have been quite that high." Dan's academic struggles were a point of high humor with the foursome.

It was an irreverent, noisy affair except for one unexpected moment. The school passed out several athletic trophies, and to his surprise, Bucky heard his name called to receive the MVP honor for varsity baseball. His fellow seniors rose to give him a standing ovation, but it died quickly as students remembered his spiritual struggle three weeks earlier.

"God stuffed the ballot box!" someone shouted from the back, and the reflective mood quickly broke as everyone laughed.

The vice principal went through the names quickly as the nearly 300 seniors paraded across the platform. Bucky felt his heart flip-flop as the Ns went forward, and Lisa accepted her diploma. She turned to wave to her mom and then blew him a big kiss.

Finally it was his turn. The PA system echoed with his full name, and he couldn't help but grin. "What a name! Who is that, Stone?" the guy behind him laughed. Bucky accepted the diploma and the handshakes of the principal and academic dean. "We're proud of you, Bucky," the administrator added. "You've brought a tremendous amount of credit to this school."

For just a moment Bucky turned to face the sea of faces. No, it hadn't been an easy four years. At times being a Christian in this very secular place had pushed him almost to the limit. But he sensed a rich reward that came from being God's man "in the world." Jesus had been able to use him here.

Moments later Mom and Dad and Rachel Marie surrounded him with hugs and presents. "You did OK, son," Dad told him. Pastor and Mrs. Jensen were both there to congratulate the Adventist graduates, and Sam gave his former classmates big hugs. "I got the room all reserved for us at PUC," he announced.

"We'll be ready."

Tracy Givenchy came up just as Bucky, Dan, Lisa, and Julie were getting ready to pose for a photo. "Congratulations, you guys," she bubbled, glancing over at Bucky.

"Hey, you too." He grinned, remembering the brief romantic fling from last year. "You got the top spot, smarty."

"Aaah, just luck." She laughed, then slipped a little card onto the top of Bucky's pile of presents. "Have fun tonight."

They posed for the shot, and a final picture of Bucky with his little sister. "Here, you wear this," he teased, putting the cap on her head.

"Do I look smart in it?"

"Yeah, sweetie." Curious, he opened the card from the red-headed senior.

"What's it say?" Lisa asked, pretending to pout.

"Hang on." He glanced at the message. *If you didn't have a new girlfriend, Mr. Stone, I'd give you a graduation kiss to remember. All the best, Tracy G.* At the bottom of the card, she had added: *With real admiration for a true MAN of God.*

He flushed, then let Lisa read it. She laughed. "It's fine except for the kissing part."

"With you here, I don't need that anyway," he responded.

"That's right." She reached up and pulled him closer as they kissed. "And don't you forget it." A trace of her perfume lingered.

Dan and Julie came over to them. "We're still going out, right?"

"Yeah." Bucky handed his pile of presents to Dad. "Can you take these home for me?"

The crowd was thinning out now, and he pulled off the mortarboard to let the evening breeze blow through his hair. Then he slipped an arm around Lisa, enjoying the closeness and silky feel of the long graduation robes as they did the slow walk out to his car. She was flushed with excitement as other students came by to wish her well.

"Ready to go?"

"Hang on a minute." She sat in the passenger seat next to him, her head resting on his shoulder, as the lights in the distance slowly blinked off one by one.